# Antonio Tabucchi

# Tristano Dies

## A LIFE

Translated from the Italian by Elizabeth Harris

*archipelago books*

First published as *Tristano Muore* by Feltrinelli in 2004.
*Tristano Muore* copyright © Giangiacomo Feltrinelli Editore Milano, 2004

Archipelago Books
232 3rd Street #A111
Brooklyn, NY 11215

www.archipelagobooks.org

Library of Congress Cataloging-in-Publication Data
Tabucchi, Antonio, 1943-2012.
[Tristano muore. English]
Tristano Dies : a life / Antonio Tabucchi ; translated from the
Italian by Elizabeth Harris. – First Archipelago Books Edition.
pages cm
ISBN 978-0-914671-24-4 (paperback)
I. Harris, Elizabeth (Translator) II. Title.
PQ4880.A24T89513 2015
853'.914—dc23     2015023969

Cover art: Pablo Picasso

The publication of *Tristano Dies: A Life* was made possible with support
from Lannan Foundation, the National Endowment for the Arts, and the
New York State Council on the Arts, a state agency.

PRINTED IN THE UNITED STATES OF AMERICA

Who bears witness for the witness?

PAUL CELAN

It's hard to contradict the dead.

FERRUCCIO

# Tristano Dies

## A LIFE

…Rosamunda Rosamunda on such a lovely evening I truly am believing it's fairy dust I'm breathing a thousand voices thousand choices thousand hearts are all rejoicing such happiness is ours such joy beneath the stars Rosamunda if you look at me Rosamunda I'll your sweetheart be… You like that one?… that's from my time, when Rosamunda looked at Tristano and the more she looked at him the more he liked her… Rosamunda if you look at me Rosamunda I'll your sweetheart be… Oh Rosamunda all of my love is for you oh Rosa-munda the more I look at you the more I like you Rosa-mu-u-u-undà… Hearts are all rejoicing such happiness is ours – not that it was so happy back then, it was cold in the mountains, frozen, really, outside, inside, I'll tell you about it, get comfortable, you've got a bit ahead of you, but not too long, don't worry, rough guess, maybe a month or so, you'll see, I'll be gone before the end of August, how was the drive?… it's not easy finding your way around here with all the twists and turns, I told Frau to be really careful giving out directions, I expected you earlier, but I'm sure she did her best to confuse you, not that her Italian isn't good – it's better than mine – been here her whole life – but when she doesn't want to do something she starts turning German, just for spite. You'll take Daphne's rooms, tell her I said so.


...You know, all told, life's more what you don't remember than what you do... Frau popped her head in, not a ripple now, she told me, where you once swam with a woman, and she shut the door again. I don't know if that was Sunday's poem or some decree... Frau gets moralistic when there's work to be done. But what work? – what's there left to do in this house, and today's not exactly Sunday, right?... You've got to have the memory of an elephant, but that's not what we men have, who knows, one day maybe they'll come up with an electronic memory, a card the size of your fingernail that they'll slip into your brain to record your entire life... Speaking of elephants, of all the creatures of this world and all their funeral rites, I've always admired elephants' the most, they have this strange way of dying – you know about it? When an elephant feels his time has come he leaves the herd, but not alone, he chooses a companion, and they leave together. They start out across the savannah, often at a trot, depending on how urgent the dying elephant is feeling... and they wander and wander, sometimes kilometers and kilometers, until the dying elephant chooses his place to die, and he goes round and round again, tracing a circle, because he knows it's time to die, he is carrying death inside him but needs to find it in space, as though he has an appointment, as though he wants to look outside himself, look death in the eye, and tell her, good morning madam death, here I am… of course it's an imaginary circle, but it helps to geograph death, if you will… and he's the only one who can enter this circle, for death is a private act, extremely private, so no one else can enter except the one who's dying… and at this point he tells his companion he can leave, goodbye, thanks so much, and the other returns to the herd… I started reading Pascal when I was a young man, I used to like him, especially his Jansenist beliefs, it was all so black and white, so clear; see, back then, in the mountains, life was black and white, your choices had to be precise, here or there, black or white, but then life teaches you the different shades of gray… But I've always liked Pascal's definition, a sphere whose center is everywhere and whose circumference is nowhere, it reminds me of the elephants… And in a way, this has something to do with why I called you here… like I said, you'll need to be patient because it's not quite my time yet, but you knew at once to trot along beside me, to accompany the one who's dying… I'm the only one who knows my circle, I know when the moment will arrive; it's true that the hour chooses us, but it's also true that you have to agree on being chosen, it's something the hour decides but in the end it's something you decide as well, as if you'd made your choice and were only giving in… For now, let's trot along together, and while it might seem we're moving forward, we're really going backward, because I'm an elephant who's called you to go backward, but I'm going back to reach my circle that's ahead. So for now, just listen and write. When the time comes for us to say goodbye, I'll let you know.

I have something to confess… after I called you I had second thoughts. I'm not sure why, maybe I don't believe in writing, writing falsifies everything, you writers are falsifiers. Or maybe it's that a person must carry his life to the grave. I mean a person's real life, the one he lives inside. What should be left to others is just the life outside, what's already plain to see, obvious. But I feel like writing my life – telling it – writing it down by proxy – you're the one doing the writing, though it's me. Strange, don't you think?

…I'd like to try and start from the beginning, if a beginning even exists, because… where does the story of a life begin, I mean, how do you decide? You can start with a fact, that's true, and so I have to pick a fact, a fact concerning this life of mine you've come to write. So I'll pick a fact. But does a fact begin with a fact? Sorry, I'm confused, I'm not sure how to explain… I mean, someone does something, and this thing determines the course of his life, but this thing he's done, it probably doesn't happen by a miracle, it's probably inside him already, and who knows how it started… Maybe a childhood memory, the glimpse of a face, a dream from long ago that you thought you'd forgotten, and here it is one day, this thing that occurs, but its origins... who can say... Tristano talked about Schubert that day in Plaka, it was winter, and in that eerie square people were lined up, bowl in hand, waiting for their *koinè* soup – you know what that is? – the swill those in charge back then gave to Greek citizens so they wouldn't starve: nasty, lukewarm water, a few shreds of potato and cabbage floating on top... variations, said Antheos, though Tristano called him Marios because he reminded him of his friend in the outskirts of Turin, the spitting image of his dear friend Marios who hid in a barn with his lover, an extraordinary woman, until thirty-nine, when he said I prefer not to, and he started his own resistance early on, meaning, before the real Resistance began, but you didn't know that for your novel... Sometimes I can't help but smile at what you thought you knew, but other than that, I liked your book, really, it's the very best testimony to that heroic time, the only heroic time we've ever known, for that matter... I'm using *testimony* loosely, because you couldn't have been there, but it feels like you were, like you were witness to a time, a choice, a moral stance... but you also got the facts down, September eighth, the Republic of Salò that cropped up again with such arrogance, like an arbiter of Italian fate, a denial of the meaning of civil war, a strong position to take these days, a bit rash, maybe, you know better than me that back then people were shooting at their enemies and friends alike, but that's not what's important, what I enjoyed about your novel is how well-informed it is on the nature of heroism, loyalty, disloyalty, of pleasure and emotions...

You're a very patient man, otherwise, considering how rude I was when you arrived, you'd have left already, said the hell with it, and this commitment you made, this book you're writing in my place, you'd chuck it all and tell me what I've got coming to me… But instead, here you sit, not moving a muscle; you're really something, writer; I don't know if you're chicken or braver than me, and that's why you put up with me… I think there's a big fly buzzing around – you hear it? – there's a buzzing in this room, really loud, is it the music of the heavens?, no, the universe isn't buzzing, it's the sound of writers, the unpleasant scratching of pens on paper, but you, you're not scratching the page, you tame the page, like a lion tamer at the circus… this heavenly music I'm talking about is truly great, the music that the angels played, the angels imagined by the painters in my Tuscany, and there's no fixed score, because there are always variations… variations, that gaunt Greek soldier told Tristano across a small café table in Plaka, while the apocalypse loomed… Variations, he said: for now, I'm just introducing variations, you see, by now, all the music's been played already, and the only thing left for us poor bastards is introducing variations, take Schubert's Impromptu Op. 142 for the piano, you know that one?, there's a sadness to it, a sadness that lays siege to the soul, that gives some idea of this occupation of yours, this siege on my homeland; there's an obsession to this music, maybe something Schubert was obsessed with, that's also present in the accompanying music to that piece titled "Rosamunde." And then Tristano gave a tired wave toward the Parthenon, as though the gods themselves had been trampled beneath the invaders' boots... and at that point a boy approached from across the square, wheeling an old bicycle beside him, skinny, just a child, bundled in an enormous military coat that dragged along the ground, his aluminum mess-kit hanging from his neck by a piece of twine, he saw the German soldiers standing watch by the line of people, and he began to whistle a tune, a partisan song with a slow, grave refrain that his whistling made sound almost cheerful, almost a march... a German approached, pointed his submachine gun at the boy who wouldn't stop, who kept walking, defiantly whistling, as if this were some sort of game, his face, teasing... everyone watching, everyone knew what was going to happen, but no one moved, no one budged, like they were all under a spell, the metallic sound of the magazine clip like a rock falling to the pavement, and the soldier fired, and the small boy crumpled to the ground, the bicycle on top of him... and then an old woman stepped out of line, her voice pierced the frozen silence of Plaka, and she screamed a curse at them, Tristano understood, it was an ancient curse of eternal damnation, the Germans along the portico heard but didn't understand her words, they understood her tone, the soldier raised his submachine gun and fired again, the woman slumped to the pavement, a figure in black, arms thrown out in agony, and Tristano, as by divine gift – no, more like divine regulation, because he had his regulation musket – aimed his gun at the German's chest, and killed him on the spot... and like magic Plaka came to life, and men appeared out of nowhere, because some unforeseen stagehand like Tristano had decided it was time for the avenging furies in this Greek tragedy to enter the scene; he didn't anticipate a revolt would break out due to something he'd done by instinct, not even thinking what might happen, but it was as though the gears had started turning on their own; through death, life had resumed at an uncontrollable pace, because that's how life is, and history's what follows, you ever think of it that way, writer?…

…Frau couldn't set you up in Daphne's rooms, there's nothing left now, just the bare walls. Don't get mad, I just wanted to see what she'd do when you asked, even if I already knew; she put you in my study, that's where she puts the guests – all of them – a government minister came once, and Frau asked me right in front of him if she should put him in my study, and his assistant, there by protocol, stared at her, scandalized, outraged, and said: the esteemed minister will return to Rome tonight… but you like my study, I know you do, you came looking for the truth and it's as if she's right there in the room beside you, in among the mold and trash… congratulations. You know what happened to the truth? She died and never found a husband.

Who understands matter's slippery ways? Scientists? You writers? You might understand how things work, but no one knows their secrets. Listen, things have an agreement among themselves that we're not privy to, a different kind of logic…

Gravity doesn't behave the way we think, and neither do the chemical combinations we studied in school, an oxygen molecule attached to two hydrogen molecules that forms the liquid we call water... you have to know the tactics of the universe, because the universe does have its tactics, but they won't show up in any lab... Newton's binomial theorem is wonderful, but there are other depths, other mysteries to mathematics. Am I waxing philosophical? Say something – no – just let me talk, all right? You intellectuals, you're always philosophizing, always explaining the world to us, everybody's always wanting to explain the world... A rose is a rose is a rose. Not true. Did you know the rose bush and the pear tree both belong to the family *Rosaceae*? Study your botany: the pear tree produces pears and the rose bush, roses; do they seem the same to you... So let me philosophize... I have so little left, you see... Please don't look at my leg – no – pull the sheet up... There's a big fly, you hear it? – it keeps hitting the mirror, stupid thing wants out, thinks the mirror's a window. I told you, don't look at my leg, it's disgusting, even if I can't see it, the way they've got me lying back against the pillows, the doctor made his ruling that the leg had to be amputated and I told him if he felt so inclined to amputate something, then he could just go ahead and cut off his own balls, but my leg, rotten as it was, was going into the grave to rot alongside the rest of me – if you please; I know it's disgusting, eaten away with gangrene, up to the groin now, in a little while everything will be eaten away, what's left of my manhood, if I don't die first, but there's not much left to chew on, my sack's empty, and this too gives me the right to philosophize as much as I see fit, it's the philosophy of someone who's all dried up, humorless, like stone… Have you seen what the world's come to, at least our world?, I'm talking about our part of the world, where we live… all gone to fat, oily, look at them, those I was talking about earlier, the windbags, they're full of humors circulating under fat… triglycerides, all cholesterol, and here I am instead, practically a mineral, see?… stones… stones don't say a thing… I'm a talking stone, a rock on a riverbank that just sits there being oh so good watching the water saying, go on, go on now, sister water, keep on flowing, who knows who you think you are, I'm staying put here on my riverbank, still as stone, because I'm a stone, brother stone… Did Frau give you a nice room? Frau's like that, she loves me but she does things out of spite, she likes being spiteful, it's what's left to an old woman, being spiteful to others; if she didn't love me so much, she'd be the same with me, and maybe she is already, and I just don't notice – we grew up together, you know – she's my same age even if she thinks she's my mother, but women are like that, they always think of themselves as your mother even when they're your same age. Put a bed in one of the rooms where Daphne stayed… when she was there… she was there such a short while, now they're just two empty rooms, her old furniture's spread all over the house now, it hurts less that way, but to Frau, her furniture's sacred, holy… you know, I think Daphne could only tolerate it here because Frau was here, because Frau loved her so… she told me once that it was thanks to Frau that she'd forgotten about hating the Germans; how do I make her understand, she said, that nothing's her fault?... You know, Frau judges everyone on sight, like they were chickens: if someone has his feathers down, she puts him in the worst chicken coop, and you come off as timid – speak up now – raise your crest, Frau notices that sort of thing, at noon insist you're staying in those rooms, you just need a bed and nightstand... from this part of the house you can see the towers of the city, they're beautiful, you seen them yet?, they almost float in the heat, it makes them tremble from below, cuts them off, lifts them, pulls them toward heaven... They're ancient towers, they seem to long for the sky, you've seen them, right?... go ahead and open the shutters a little, see if you can get rid of that big fly – you hear it? – it keeps hitting the mirror, it's so stupid, it thinks the mirror's a way out... Look at the towers of the city, the surrounding hills, this landscape I'm leaving behind, look at it for me. And from this part of the house you can hear the cicadas, from the back you can't hear them, the cicadas sing outside the entire afternoon, I like their little concert, their simple music, castanets and cymbals... I've returned here to leave, returned to where I was born, to hear my cicadas, that I used to listen to on summer afternoons when I was little and they'd send me in for my siesta and I entertained myself with the cicadas, and with books to explain the world, as if books could explain the world... Dreams... Why did I ask for you in particular? You know why: because I liked your book, I'd already been the inspiration for another novel, you know that better than me, but it was so close to what happened, it was so realistic it seemed false, but I didn't phone you so you'd record me, I don't want my voice to remain – besides, that's too easy – what sort of writer would that make you? Write it down, if you can; I want to remain in written words, and if you can't write it down now, then record it in your mind, mentally record it, and then write it in your own words, like I know you can, someone tells you one thing, and you write it so it seems like something else… Tell Frau to come give me my morphine, and then you should come back later, the last one's worn off, the pain's making me complain, and I don't want to complain – too depressing… Did I already tell you about Vanda? I can't remember…

…They saw a dog, but that had to be a different day, who knows when, late in their life together, anyway. The dog's name was Vanda – not with a w, just a v, a begging mutt like that. The dog didn't tell them its name, it couldn't, it couldn't even pant any more, but Rosamunda remembered, when she saw the dog up ahead. Look, a dog – it's Vanda – you remember? They almost hit her – it was dark in the tunnel and they were rounding a curve. Once out of the tunnel, on the straightaway, they pulled to the side to wait, to avoid being rear-ended by a truck, which can happen; Vanda appeared, limping along, head drooping, tongue down to the asphalt, but she was off to the right, well clear of the white line. Her teats swung low, like she'd been nursing, nursing a litter, though this wasn't possible: just from her lips and teeth, she looked to be at least twenty, even older, which was fine for a person but decrepit for a dog. It's because she's so kindhearted, one of them said, I don't remember who, Vanda's good, a good girl, she's spent her life buried up to the neck. They hauled her onto the back seat, the pads of her paws were raw from her journey. They knew she'd gone a thousand kilometers for them to find her, though they didn't say it, some things you just don't say; a being has to drill through layers and layers of time, pulling round itself the bits and pieces necessary in order to take shape, until it breaks the surface, a living creature, though perhaps already dying, like Vanda, so fucked from the start, thinking it's about to start, when it's already arrived. Christ, he said, what's the point? A rhetorical question… It was noon and very hot and the sun was blinding – the Mediterranean sun. When things like this happen, it's always very hot, the sun's always blinding, and it has to be Mediterranean – that's a well-known fact. So well-known, you can believe it or not, your choice. And if you feel like believing it, at that moment he was driving slowly, the rocky coast stretched out, reddish, the strip of sea, a deep blue. Vanda seemed to be sleeping, but she wasn't, she had one eye closed, one eye open, fixed upon the back car door and the ashtray full of butts, as if this ashtray were the meager aleph she'd been granted and in this, her universe of butts, she might discover the sick god who'd created her, the sinister mysteries of his religion. Glancing back at her, he could see the question in her fearful eye, the pupil dilated, and he whispered, the father's a dark turn, the son's those spat-out cigarette butts, and the holy spirit's a time long gone by now – there's your holy trinity, dear Vanda, accept your fate – there's nothing you can do. You never wanted children, Rosamunda said, and she seemed to be speaking to the slight haze of heat dancing on the horizon, all those years, your sperm always left on my belly, thrown away, and now my Vanda's been born, but it's late, too late. She'll die tomorrow, he said, but keep her tonight, rock her like she's your child, offer her your breast, if you want, it's better than nothing, I threw my sperm away because you lied, so I lied, too… What a strange night, in Taddeo's *Zimmer*. Framed by the window, two ships sliding by, lit up, silent, dreamlike. Only afterwards, when the ships had moved beyond the frame, did they catch a handful of notes on the wind, weak notes, maybe a waltz. Were they dancing on board? Not out of the question: there's often dancing on board a ship, especially on a cruise, even a short, cheap Sunday cruise like the one that crosses from San Fruttato to San Zaccarino and lasts for only a day. As soon as they can, the people on board start dancing, you have to take advantage of the time you have to enjoy yourself, especially if you bought the ticket, because Monday comes soon enough. Rosamunda tried to offer Vanda her breast, but she wouldn't nurse. They heard her weak breathing almost till dawn, then it stopped. They buried her there, on the beach, in a pocket-sized cove full of pebbles where a path drops down to the water's edge, the small waves washing over pebbles, over them again, century after century. With shells and small stones, Rosamunda spelled out Vanda zero zero zero zero on the grave, those zeros referring to the day she was born and the day she died, and also, as Tristano alone would know, filling them with the time gone by from the day Rosamunda had begun to desire a child to that day when her desire had been buried beneath the body of an old dog, because bit by bit, desires also die and wind up buried underground. They stayed to watch the sun rise over that sliver of horizon between two promontories, in that charming seaside resort, which they'd been to other times by bus. The sun was quite strong, and they both understood without speaking, because everything under the sun is old, sometimes very old. Which doesn't diminish anyone's suffering, including theirs. Sing me something, she said softly, like you used to. Like what? he asked. Like when we were up in the mountains and you carried me on the handlebars of your bicycle, and you sang to me, remember?, I leaned my head on your chest and while you sang, I caught whiffs of garlic – we ate so much garlic in the mountains! – but maybe that was another time, when we ate escargot à la provençal, we'd eat escargot à la provençal, we'd treat ourselves, and those were full of garlic, too. He sang, the olive falls, no leaves fall, your beauty won't ever, you're like the sea of waves that grows with wind, but with water, never. It was a lullaby. Hard to say if it was to rock Vanda toward her final nothing, or if it was for them, or for their never-ending dreams.


...It opens with... wait, let me think... it goes: I saw some girls screaming in the storm, the wind carried their words away then brought them back again, and I – coward – heard these words but didn't understand that maybe they were telling me my youth had died… that's how it goes, but it's too long, one of those things Frau tortures me with on Sundays, maybe I'll recite some more, when it comes to me, we've got plenty of time… I told Frau, Renate, have a heart, don't read me poems like that on Sunday, can't you see what state I'm in? – how about something lighter, something from our childhood, like March sprinkles tinkling silver on the eaves, please, Renate, something like that, okay? It's August, she says, it's ungodly hot down here – it's August, young sir – what do March sprinkles have to do with anything?


Her name was Daphne, but he also called her Mavri Elià, for her big eyes like two black olives. It happened that day in Plaka, the Nazi officer lay sprawled out, legs apart, in the middle of the square, a few meters from the boy and woman he'd killed, a thread of blood trickling from his mouth; a group of Germans came running down the narrow lane leading from the Columns of Zeus, the headquarters were in the Hotel Grande Bretagne, someone started firing out the windows overlooking the square – Greek partisans – bullets chipped Aeolus's Column, bullets carried by the wind, Tristano pulled off his Italian military jacket and tossed it to the pavement, by the dead Nazi, because he didn't want to get shot by partisans, but mostly because he didn't want to be Italian anymore, didn't want that horrible cloth next to his skin, that cloth of an invading soldier sent by a mad, grim reaper who wanted to rip Greece's heart out on the shore… She emerged from behind a green front door; Tristano saw a small door open in that massive one, and she stepped out like a small, stray animal; she looked around, confused, she walked into the square, hesitated, saw Tristano nearby, stared at him with those enormous dark eyes. I'm an Italian soldier, he said. I just killed a German officer. She didn't understand, and Tristano poked himself in the chest and repeated, Italian. And then he made his finger and thumb into a pistol, which he pointed at the Nazi lying on the ground, and he said, bang, and blew on his finger. She started to go back, and she gestured that he should follow her inside. Why am I telling you this, writer?… I don't know, a writer like you doesn't need this sort of episode… or maybe you do… you're not a writer who looks down his nose at sentiment, when it's there, that's why I'm telling you this… Tristano followed her, and she shut the door. She looked at him with those enormous bewildered eyes, disbelieving, maybe she was frightened – he was the enemy. Tristano told her his name, his nickname as a boy, Ninototo. She said in Greek, I'm Daphne, and Tristano smiled as though he'd forgotten what was happening all around them, and he said he'd learned a little Greek with the invasion: I only know how to use the infinitive, but I to call you Mavri Elià because your eyes to be black olives. She gestured that he should follow, and they climbed the ancient stairway, the ceiling was vaulted, and against the walls stood amphora vases encrusted with barnacles, and on the walls hung dark paintings of solemn, bearded men. She led him through empty rooms around an inside courtyard. They didn't speak. He was shivering, she said something he didn't understand, meanwhile the sun had pierced the grayness of the day, a sunbeam cut through the silent rooms, there was gunfire, but it seemed far, far away, they came to an enormous room, almost bare, with only a small bed, an icon above it, a mirror, and a piano. She spoke to him in French. She said, this room, it's mine, and now it's yours. And then she said in her own language, *efharisto*. And she started to go. Thank you for what? he asked. For killing my enemy, she said. I'm the enemy, too, Tristano said. She smiled, she sat down on the edge of that small bed with a flowered shawl for a bedspread, and she said, who are the two of us, really? She was smiling, and her eyes had a sweetness to them that you can't imagine, writer, even if you're a writer who's good at describing women, you'll never get at that sweetness, it was just as inconceivable to Tristano, that Italian soldier, that invader who had no idea why he'd just killed a Nazi officer, an ally of his country, nothing seemed to make any sense to him. And you know what? – nothing did make sense back then, and that's the truth. Tristano felt very uneasy, and his heart was pounding, too much emotion that day for a boy his age, you can imagine, writer, seeing how you toy with others' emotions. He slipped closer to the window overlooking the square, cautious, peering through the lace curtains at the bodies of the woman and boy still lying on the pavement; the Germans had managed to drag the dead officer past the Tower of the Winds, but no one was around, not one living soul, a suspended moment, like in an empty theater, there was only a motorcycle with a sidecar, a soldier slumped over the handlebars, his helmet on crooked, probably the poor bastard they first sent out to recover the body, but a Greek sniper got him. She left him alone in that room. He studied himself in the mirror, he was young then, Tristano was, but he seemed like an old man. He looked at the sheet music on the piano: a piece by Schubert. He stretched out on the bed, in that room that was so Franciscan for such a palatial house, a modest room, with a dirty mirror and a bed that would see so much love… But he didn't think that – I'm only telling you this because Frau read me yet another poem. Do you recognize that one? Tristano didn't, but he understood that the Franciscan simplicity of the room was the only way to counter the squalor of that life and that world; he rose, and as if he were sleepwalking, he stretched his arms in front of him, almost to protect himself from the disgust that had settled over this time in which he was living, that had settled over everything, he moved toward the dark hallway, and he shouted, Mavri Elià! Mavri Elià, we have to save each other! Then he lay down on the small bed and closed his eyes. She tiptoed in so he didn't even hear, *vous m'avez appelée?* she asked. Please, Tristano said, please play me some Schubert, what's there on the piano. She sat down to begin. Tristano stopped her. You know that theme Schubert used as the accompaniment in "Rosamunde?" Then they made love the entire night, silently, as if this were something necessary, natural. In the morning, he held her while she spoke of Saint George's face on a Byzantine icon found on one of the Aegean Islands, I don't remember which one. I think he told her about a Romanesque cathedral in his hometown that had an enormous rose window, and half-asleep, almost delirious, he told her about a rose of the winds and that the only thing to do in life was follow the winds, Aeolus, he kept saying, Aeolus… It was dawn. Tristano got up and peeked through the curtains at the square. It was deserted. All that was down there by the Tower of the Winds were the bodies of the boy and woman in black, along with the German soldier slumped over his sidecar motorcycle. Tristano went to her and kissed her closed eyes, spoke into her ear, Mavri Elià, he said, I've found you and I'll never let you go, I'm taking you away with me, you know what we're going to do? – it's dawn, we're getting out of here, we'll block out the cold with the tapestries from this old house, you're getting in the sidecar, I'm getting on the motorcycle, and we're going to Piraeus, the allies are there, they'll take us away, we'll make it to my home, that's where the head of the serpent lies, and that's where he has to be fought, we have to crush his head, otherwise his poison will spread everywhere, I'm going to crush his head and I'm taking you with me, we're going to cross this city under siege and make it to the sea, and why not – it's no more absurd than this absurdity all around us… She opened her eyes, maybe she heard what Tristano was whispering in his sleep, or maybe not, and she gave him a smile that was just as lost. If I can, I'm taking you to another Principate, Tristano said, but luckily, that one's dying, they told me it was dying, so at least we'll be stepping out of the fire and into the frying pan.

…Of course that's not how it went – you probably knew that already. But you should write it down like it was real, because it was certainly real for Tristano, and what's important is what he imagined his entire life, till it turned to memory. Yes, he really did kill the Nazi soldier, and Daphne really did take him into that old house and play Schubert for him and stare at him with those big, dark eyes. But they never came close to touching each other, she only spoke to him about her violated country and at dawn she had him sneak out in her father's over-coat, and he never went to Piraeus at all, he only reentered Italy after September eighth, two of Daphne's friends took him as far as Corinth, where he joined the Greek partisans in the Peloponnese Mountains. And when he slipped outside the door that morning, he whispered to her, I'm coming back, Daphne – I swear it – please, wait for me.

I don't know what it could mean, why I'm so sad, I find a fairytale from times unseen won't vanish from my mind… That was yesterday's poem, in German, sometimes Frau behaves as though we've returned to childhood, there seems to be a little arteriosclerosis going around. Now, young sir, here's Sunday's poem, she tells me. It's a ritual from the past, she likes following orders, she does. It was my grandfather's order when he sent for her, so I'd learn the language. Our ritual went like this: I sat in the armchair in the living room for fifteen minutes before the lesson began, because children must wait, a quarter to five, my grandfather didn't compromise on schedules, on everything else, yes, but because of a schedule, he'd say, some people missed the boat for Calatafimi; on the little end table there was the pot of hot chocolate and two cups, one for me and one for Frau, I wore knickers, knock knock, and then *Guten Abend Herrchen, Entschuldigung*, it's poetry time, she was a little girl, my age, yes, Fräulein, she was shy back then, Frau was, and I was even shyer, she was embarrassed to read and I to listen, she avoided looking at me, I avoided looking at her, Frau, she loved me, even if she can be spiteful, and in my way, I love her, too; as you well know, she's the only one with me now, if you think about it, we've spent our whole lives avoiding looking at each other, maybe because we wanted so badly to look at each other back when we were children and we never got up the nerve… *Ich weiss nicht was soll es bedeuten, Dass ich so traurig bin, Ein Märchen aus alten Zeiten*… You know that one? German children learn it in elementary school, it's about a siren, a blond creature sitting on a rock along the Rhine, and with her golden hair and singing, she seduces sailors, and they shipwreck, Lorelei, she's called… Frau always started up like this again, every time I returned, as if nothing had changed, an empty ritual, but it still had to be honored because of a contract from years ago, a life's work to fulfill, even if her language changed over the years, different poems, different accents, but always the same shell of a ritual, Frau knows it's her right and she takes advantage of it, she picks the poems, she's always picked them, and that's as it should be, she knows, she knows so many things, Frau does, she knows the hours, the days of my life, like a book of hours that the monks used so long ago… life passes in a breath, you know, but sometimes a Sunday afternoon can go by so slowly, and Frau has always known how to pick just the right poem for the right time – when I was home, of course, because I often wasn't – I was almost never home, in fact – but you know what she told me? She told me something troubling, almost moving, it's strange, because feelings are for those with humors left in the bottle, and a mineral like me no longer holds moisture, but when she told me in her terse way, in that rasping Italian of hers that she's always pretended not to know very well even after more than seventy years of living here, I had to turn my head toward the shutters to keep her from seeing that this stone wasn't completely dry, and the slats of the shutters started trembling, and not because it was so hot outside but because she told me, surly as usual, that even when I was far away, or in danger, or when she thought I was in danger, that every Sunday at a quarter to five, she went into the living room, she imagined pouring hot chocolate into two cups, and she'd say to herself in German, now, young sir, it's poetry time. And she'd read the poem she thought was right for me that day, like a viaticum or a book of hours… So many hours, writer, so very many. How many Sundays must there be in seventy, no, nearly eighty years? – count them. I'd guess thousands… Get me a glass of water, but rinse it out first, Frau's always adding a little hops, and I get even more dazed, take the water from the bathroom sink, it's that door by the wardrobe, sorry to make you my nurse – no, not that door, that's to the dressing room – the one to the right – you have to push a little, the door knob sticks, it's the faucet with the red handle, the blue one's hot water, the plumber screwed up putting them in and I never got them reversed, are you by any chance looking at the photograph in my dressing room?... I bet you are, since you're not answering, please, don't let it make you feel uncomfortable, I don't want that, photos like that can make a person uncomfortable, they're embarrassing, even after so many years, that body's real, though, even if it's imitating a painting, trying to imitate a Courbet, there's a yellow stain almost up to the navel, a devouring hand, like my gangrene, photos keep up with us, we grow wrinkled, they turn yellow, deteriorate, they have skin like ours, you know, skin preserves that internal sea we're made of, because we're made of water, it protects the body from external heat while at the same time holding our heat inside, getting rid of any excess, depending on the season... and when the sea has evaporated, the shell remains, shriveled, useless... That shot was taken with a Leica I got off a German officer; in his jacket, by his pistol, he carried a photo of his family and also his precious Leica, he loved his own family even if he slaughtered the families of others, it's human to love your own family, that photo has to be from forty-eight, or maybe a little before that, when Tristano found *Guagliona* again, that's what I feel like calling her today, just *girl*, they wound up at a sort of pensione, by accident, everything in life happens by accident, at times I think even free will is just an accident… how strange, can you believe that I remember exactly what we ate – *cacciucco* – fish stew – and I can't remember if we made love, but he suggested to her that she pose like the origin of the world, that's the truth, the proof's in that sorry photo, it was a late summer afternoon, the light was low, beautiful; Rosamunda, Tristano said, let's do the origin of the world… but for them there was no origin of the world, they didn't originate a damn thing, a sterile love, I'd say, with no transmission of the flesh… well, it's better that way, besides… This water's warm, I told you the faucets are reversed, cold water's on the right, and next time, put in the straw that's there on the nightstand, otherwise I drench the sheet, see, I can't really swallow, I can't lap up water like a dog… I was telling you about Frau, last Sunday she read me a poem, seemed like a nice one… Last night I had a good dream, I entered the origin of the world… but whose?… bring me a little more water, but get the straw… dreams are pretty wretched miracles… I've never believed in real miracles… the real ones are illusions… especially dreams. Sunday was the day before yesterday, right? – I've lost track of time – there's Frau, knocking quietly like she used to seventy-five years ago, now, it's poetry time, young sir. She sits down, opens a book… Sunday… Frau understands Sundays, she's one of those people in life who understands Sundays, she tries to clear her voice, which isn't possible, by now she sounds like a bellows, she puffs when she speaks, emphysema, the doctor was clear about that, but she pretended not to understand, Frau's incredible, if you tell her something she doesn't like, then she makes sure she's a German just off the boat, she sneaks cigars, smokes them, hiding out in the vineyard, Agostino's nephew told me, he does the tilling, which is useless in that diseased vineyard; professor, sir, he says, madam Frau will sit under the poplar at the back of the vineyard, and she'll smoke three Toscano cigars, one after the other, every day she's there, from three to five, I thought you should know – it's a bit shocking. And what's she doing while she smokes? I asked. Nothing, Agostino's nephew says, staring off into the distance, looking lost; I walked right past her and she didn't even notice, or she pretended not to. She must be thinking back to when she was a girl in Germany, I told him; don't you ever think back to when you were a child? – sure you do, but it's easier because you're at home and you were a child here, so don't concern yourself with her, let her smoke all the cigars she wants, even people who don't have anyone have to think about some-one… I heard a buzzing, something on my face, must be that big fly. Maybe if you cracked the shutters, it could find its way out, but just a crack now – too much light – that light seems to make my leg hurt even more… Frau read me a poem by a poet I don't know, must be a poetess instead of a poet, right? – if the poet's female she's a poetess, right? – oh, it doesn't matter – young sir, she tells me, Sunday's poem, and she begins… this quiet dust. I know that one by heart, I said, it's American, and has always filled me with regret. No, she says, this one's Italian, it just has the same title, but it's already five to five, we're ten minutes late… Renate, I said, how on earth is it possible, you're really something, so much time's gone by since we were children, all the time in the world, and everything time brings with it, hunger, war and famine, our own disasters, and especially the dead, everyone's dead, Renate, we're the only ones left, and you come in here and tell me we're ten minutes late – but late for what? – just be patient. For your morphine, she says firmly, and even though I can barely see right now, I sense her stubborn expression, her white hair a halo, with her loose bun… For your morphine: the doctor said you should get it every eight hours, the next one's in five minutes, so there's hardly any time, and I want to read your five o'clock poem before you can't understand a word of it. So go ahead, Renate – read. And she: where's my child, where's my roe deer? He'll come just three more times, then never come again. Renate, I said, please, no nursery rhymes. That's just how it starts, she says, now be quiet and listen… the dead are cold to the touch, but the living are something else again, when I touched my love I was happy, yesterday I had a vision, my love was in the garden, he was half-man, half-child… I can't remember the rest, Frau was reading and while she read, she gave me my morphine, I didn't notice, and so I wound up in a dream world, and I entered the origin of the world, sometimes a person's lucky and gets to dream what he wants to dream, but that's rare, a rare privilege, maybe I'll tell you my dream, if it stays with me, but later: now, I'm tired. What time is it?

Ferruccio said you mustn't tell your dreams or you'll give away your soul. I always paid attention to him, but with you, I don't think that's the case, you've come to hear my life, come all this way, dropped everything, you also deserve my dreams… I want to tell you about a beach, I don't know if I just dreamed it or if I dreamed it over the years, but that's all relative, I'll tell you about it later, because I think I found a thread of logic, and I don't want to lose it, it's so tenuous… I don't know how Frau holds on so tight. Imagine, since I've come back she's resumed this ritual from when we were children, when she taught me German, with her Sunday poem… like it was yesterday and life hadn't gone by in the meantime…

…And in the meantime the years went by, long years, all the same, the same bombs year after year, on trains, in piazzas, in banks… I'm skipping ahead, I'm already getting to the end, I want to be there already, though I can't get much closer than this… and it's all the same, like I was saying, trials all the same, defendants all the same, in the sense that there weren't any – defendants – there were trials but no defendants, strange, right? – in a democracy what's important is what's on the outside, what's on the inside doesn't matter in the least, it's the ritual that counts, and if there aren't any defendants, well, who gives a shit?… everything exactly the same, all the same smiles, oh, all the same enormous smiles around that table of world powers where we were told we had a seat… all of them, puffed up like roosters, spouses at their sides, because this was the stuff of ceremony, no joke, extremely selective places, embassies, delegations, homes, estates… especially estates, with this minister and that and heads of state and prelates and entrepreneurs and special correspondents and direct envoys, Sunday and every other day, and the banquets… first-rate, delicious, and hanged bankers or bankers to hang, and poisoned bankers or bankers to poison, and some terrorist monks, every once in a while, a nice big crack, crr-aack, and so-called civilization advanced some more, chipping away with its tiny teeth, like a stubborn creature inside the oak, crr-aack, my god what a century, said the rats, gnawing at the framework… that's what Tristano was thinking, delirious, maybe, but like I told you, I'm getting toward the end, and it isn't right to end here, otherwise why'd I call for you, just to write the end? But the fact is, when Tristano and Daphne returned, after everything that had happened, he started watching the years go by from his little Malafrasca, the name he'd given to this hill where the olive trees were turning yellow and the vineyard had grown infested… sometimes he thought he was the one who'd brought the phylloxera to the vineyard, he confessed to Daphne… don't be so hard on yourself, she whispered, coming close, while Tristano, a lost look in his eyes, stared off over the plains, to the sun dying on the horizon, and she caressed his neck, like she was stroking the keys on her piano, don't think about your fine wine and extra-virgin olive oil – it was a wonderful idea, that farm you wanted so long ago, those ideas you had were all wonderful, but they weren't for you, they weren't important, not really, our books are what's important, our Hypnos Pages, they were your real dream, and now they exist, and they'll live on, you left our boy the land, you loved it vicariously, you wanted someone to love it in your stead because you were born here, grew up here, that's understandable, you wanted it to go on, but life was bitter and the branch broke, still, you've got your Daphne here with you, stop thinking about these vineyards and these olives… But Tristano wasn't thinking about the land; he was looking past the crowns of the trees with their suffering olives, he was looking toward the horizon and thinking of this country that he'd picked up a rifle for, wondering if it had been worth it, and his eyes wandered, settled on a canvas director's chair that Daphne had given him as a joke one year for his birthday, and on the back of the chair she'd used a marker to write the Scarlett O'Hara line, after all, tomorrow is another day, so he wouldn't be the director of a bitter wide-screen film as seen from the porch, but he thought, after all, some things in life are worth the effort, if the spirit's not suffering from the rickets; you have to fight off the rickets on certain days, when the spring seems to have dried up, because then all at once the water will start to spout, you weren't expecting it at all and there it is, so beautiful, gushing cold water, surrounding you, reviving you, sweeping you along, where did that karstic river come from, with the plains so dry, what twists and turns did that river have to make below ground before reaching you and telling you that after all, tomorrow is another day? But in the meantime he was staring off at the plains, which in cinemascope were so fertile and to him looked so dry, the land, the vineyards, and the industrial farms, and those still owned by families, lands as far as the eye could see, mostly owned now by Germans and Americans, with the occasional exception for some local aristocrat, to keep up tradition, or pretend to, and the most annoying were the Pontormos, not so much for their fine wine, which was a farce, anyway, he thought, but because they'd stolen the portrait of his favorite painter for their label and made a pop version of it, in the style of that sinister-looking American painter… But now I'm rambling, and this stuff isn't very interesting, if you really think about it, nothing here is all that interesting, except maybe one thing, meaning, the riddle, only maybe I don't feel like telling you the riddle, when I think about it, you've told the riddle of Tristano better than I ever could, it's all so clear in your book, why should I interrupt the sermon?… Anyway, I'm tired now, and you must be tired, too; I think I'll take a little nap, maybe I'll call you in later with this bell I had installed, rings all over the house, this room, too – want to hear it? – it croaks, sounds like a toad – not on purpose – that's just a coincidence, the electrician told me it's because he dropped the celluloid amplifier, and it cracked… you made Frau give you a nice room, right?, like I told you, don't take her first offer, ask to switch, she never gives anyone the best room right away, not out of spite, it's just her nature, I think there's a big fly, can you hear it, too, or is that just my own ears buzzing?

Badum badum, badum badum, *elle avait des yeux des yeux d'opale qui me fascinaient, qui me fascinaient, il y avait l'ovale de son visage pâle de femme fatale qui me fut fatal…* you hear the little birds, how they're chirping? – today I'm chirping, too, I'm feeling cheerful, it's cooler out, you can feel it, the wind's up, *on s'est connu, on s'est reconnu, on s'est perdu de vue, on s'est reperdu de vue, on s'est retrouvé, on s'est réchauffé, puis on s'est séparé…* Days like this, writer, you should head to this beach I know, take off your shirt that's whipping around you, it's the first *Libeccio* wind of the season, not too strong yet, gusts ruffling your hair, a few short steps from the pine woods, and you're on the sandy shore, your face moist with the salt water, you can lick your lips, they taste of… the sun so strong, oh, the longing, you feel it in your groin, it aches, so hot, everything burning, the sun, the sand, your gut, the beach is deserted – where is she?… *Je me suis réveillé en sentant ses baisers sur mon front brûlant, ses baisers sur mon front brûlant*, badum, badum… you look to the horizon, squint your eyes against the sun, not a soul in sight, take off your clothes, go on, leave them on the shore – Giuditta! You call out to her, the pine trees answer back – Giudittaaa! It's me, Giuditta! It's me, Giuditta! I want you, Giuditta! I want you, Giudittaaa!… *on s'est connu, on s'est reconnu, on s'est perdu de vue, on s'est reperdu de vue, on s'est séparé, puis on s'est réchauffé*, badum badum, badum badum, *chacun pour soi est riparti dans le tourbillon de la vie*, badum badum… your testicles are small and hard like two walnuts, stupid, useless testicles, and meanwhile he's hard as a club – Giuditta! – you feel like dancing, you spread wide your arms… *je l'ai revue, un soir la-la-la, elle est retombée dans mes bras, elle est retombée dans mes bras…* that dance floor of a beach so huge, in your arms once more, back in your arms, and now you're dancing and she's dancing with you, silly girl, you're here finally, I couldn't take it anymore, I really couldn't take it, it's been like that for an hour, it hurts almost, I couldn't take it anymore, let's go up to that mountain village, to Sassète, she says, the pistou festival's going on right now, I don't give a damn about pistou, you say, let's go into the beach hut, the shed in the shade, the shaded shed, badum badum, but was that beach really in Provence? – what do you think, writer – was it a beach in Provence?… maybe yes, maybe no, I could be wrong, it doesn't matter, today I'm cheerful as a little bird, you hear the birds chirping? Meanwhile, they go inside the beach hut, they don't even need to lay out a towel, the sand's a little warm, but it's cool inside the shed, oh, Cary, Cary, she says. She hugs you. You kill me, Cary. Silly Giuditta, what were you doing someplace else? – why were you so late coming back?… *on s'est connu, on s'est reconnu…* such a silly Giuditta – and why are you calling me Cary? I'm not Cary, Cary was your uncle. Oh, yeah, that's right, Clark, you always wanted to be called Tristano, yes, like that, Tristano, enough, no, yes, keep going, badum badum, badum badum, *quand on s'est connu, quand on s'est reconnu, pourquoi se perdre de vue? et quand on s'est retrouvé, quand on s'est réchauffé, pourquoi se séparer?…* Do you know why, writer? You don't and I don't, either, how could you know, when you don't know anything about Tristano, but you know what? – I feel it here, right here, the same urgency from that day – right here, where I'm being eaten away by gangrene, yes, right here in the groin, the same desire I felt back then... do you think that's crazy? You must think that's crazy, but it's not – right here – the same desire I felt back then, just the same, though as for the rest, there's nothing left, that's all been extinguished along with my dead flesh, but the same desire's still there... the desire's remained while the flesh is gone, you couldn't possibly understand, how could you understand, you, what do you know, you, about someone else's body, about my body?

...What day is it? No, I'm not dead yet, my eyes were closed but I'm not dead yet, you'll have to be patient... Today I'm feeling clear-headed, my fever must be down, no more nightmares. Have I told you some of my nightmares? If I have, don't throw anything away, everything remains in a life, especially a hero's life, even nightmares... I'm wheezing a little, you hear it?, when I breathe, there's a whistling in my throat, but don't worry, today's not the day, this thing's going to take a while, you'll just have to be patient, like me. What day is it? Let me know when it's August tenth, don't forget, but maybe the tenth's already past. I've slept so much, I must have slept so much. But maybe not... sometimes years can go by in a single minute of sleep... Frau's being stingy with the morphine, the bitch... or maybe she thinks the injections hurt, poor thing... At times, memories seem like gelatin, everything seems melded together, boneless, melting, you see a face... stop, you say, got you, you silly girl, don't you know me? – it's me – can't you tell? – it's me, wait a second... she's smiling at you... Ah, now you know me, you say, but she's sneering at you, nah nah, cutie pie, and she winks... her eyelashes, so long, and that malicious smile of hers is just the same, but the mouth's different, how strange, and her face, too, like warm wax molding itself over, into a different face now. And this one, what does he want? Ah, it's Sirio, you recognize him, it's Sirio, who died of ass cancer... but Sirio's only there a second, now it's Cary, that American commander who was with you in the mountains, you can see him so clearly, Tristano, too, you can see him like he's someone else, when he was Commander Clark, deep down they were the same person, united by skin, twin brothers, they called him that because he looked like a movie star from back then, with that stray wisp of hair, shiny with brilliantine, on his forehead, the only thing missing was the pencil mustache. And on that day, that pale morning, at dawn, he's waiting, hiding behind the boulder, he has his submachine gun aimed and ready, but he's smiling like he's got a joke for you... and you smile back; it's strange ending up like this, after all this time, and he's still there, in that same place, on that pale dawn. Maybe he never moved at all? Maybe. Men don't move, they stay put, entranced in fixed moments, only they don't realize this; we think that there's a steady, evaporating flow, but no: somewhere out there is a fixed moment, a frozen gesture, as if everything's under a spell, a photograph without a plate, without a negative. You have to know it to see it, but I'm telling you, it's there.

…So anyway, here's how it went: he saw her from a distance in the meadow, she was outside the farmhouse, turned away from him, and he set down the telescope he was carrying – he hadn't brought a weapon into the mountains. It was a miracle. She was wearing boots, a pair of knee-length leather shorts, and had a submachine gun over her shoulder, the gun barrel poking into her loose dark hair. He started trembling. From surprise, emotion, something I can't describe, a flame bursting in his chest, temples pounding. Daphne! he called. She didn't turn around. She was talking with someone, looked like a soldier in a Savoy uniform. Daphne! he called again and started running. She heard, turned around, gripping her gun. She stared at him, surprised, intense blue eyes slightly scornful, maybe because she was a little nearsighted. My name is Marilyn, she said. What do you want? She couldn't have been more than twenty, but she spoke like someone accustomed to being in charge. I'm new, he stammered, I was in Greece. I work with the allies' contacts, she said. I'm American. You can call me Captain – Captain Mary. Rosamunda suits you better, he said. Cut it out, she said. Who's Rosamunda? A piece by Schubert, he said.

Frau wanted to put the pendulum clock on the nightstand for me – at least then you'll know the time, she says, just turn your head, and you'll be less confused during the day – you're always asking the time. I told her the tick tock was annoying, but she just won't quit. No one can hear it when it's under that glass bell, she says, not even someone with tuberculosis. Someone with tuberculosis, no, but me, yes, I hear everything… I can hear a worm gnawing inside the wardrobe, it's unbearable, like a voice in a cave… the wardrobe's chestnut, worms like chestnut wood, and the more seasoned, the better, I know all about these worms… that's exactly what I told her, I know all about these worms, Renate, go on, take a look at my leg… and I know all about these sounds, too, I've got a direct line to down below, I'm hooked in, I can hear the ants crawling on little hair feet. You're getting too much morphine, she snaps – ants, nothing – this is your third injection today, but if the clock on the nightstand's annoying, then you'll just have to be patient: now that you have someone here listening to you all day long, you can ask him what time it is – I'm too busy. Too busy… what she's so busy with is a mystery, Agostino's wife does the housework, we get our supplies delivered… what she's so busy with is giving orders to anyone in reach. Does she order you around, too? Anyway, if I'm disoriented during the day, it's better at night, there's a plane – I don't know if you've heard it yet – maybe not – you must be asleep at midnight, and it's pretty high up, it sounds so far away, it's the midnight plane, that's what I call it… it's punctual, maybe just slightly late at times, not much, it strikes midnight better than that stupid clock that doesn't chime anymore, that just goes tick tock… you can see it from your bedroom window, but you have to wait for it: if you hear it, it's already passed over, you'll see it, two small blue parallel lights… that plane's been passing over for at least ten years now, I first noticed it the same evening we came back to this house, we were exhausted when we got here, you know, we'd set out that August afternoon from a small square in Plaka where Daphne as a joke had started floating overhead by an orange tree, while I begged her not to make me go alone, and so we set off on our journey… that night I couldn't sleep, which happens when you're too tired, I was at the window, you know how it is, a cigarette… That plane comes from the South and heads west, and when it's overhead, just over the house, it turns for the coast… and then he's over the sea… I can see him, he's over Sardinia, a traveler who probably sees the lights below from his small window and asks himself who's living in those lights, who's down there, in that house, that village… it's impossible to know, just like I don't know who this traveler is who's asking himself this, and yet we're both imagining this, he and I, and not knowing who we are, we've thought the same thing… and there he is, over Spain… maybe he'll even pass over Pancuervo, and in Pancuervo there'll be someone awake at midnight, staring up at that plane… and finally, over Portugal… and then it's the ocean, oh, it's true, there's nothing else for it, dear boy, you have to cross the Atlantic… and all at once you're in America, because you can reach America quickly by plane. America… My father always dreamed of going to America, my grandfather would tell me this, that my father thought he could continue his research there, in America, he could become a world-famous biologist… America… The America my father dreamed of must have been so beautiful! He knew everything about the plains, about the Seminole Indians, Benjamin Franklin, Charlie Chaplin, Walt Whitman, the Empire State Building, the music… my grandfather told me about this, too, how no one here appreciated that music, they thought it was awful, this negro music… idiots… but my father had a phonograph, and he had records shipped directly from America… it was my grandfather who taught me to love that music, after my father died, by that time, I'd lost interest in my grandfather's Garibaldi sword, and so he had to invent a new Sunday-morning game: you'd tiptoe into my father's study, as if he were in there, eye glued to his microscope and couldn't be disturbed, and then my grandfather would put on a record of someone playing the trumpet, and he'd grow very animated, twirl his white mustache to the beat, listen to him, he'd say, listen to him blow that horn, how alive it is, breath is life, kid, in the beginning was the word, and the priests, I don't know who they think they are, but the word is breath, kid, it's only breathing… life, you've got to love life and always enjoy it – remember that – the fascists are the ones who enjoy death… Writer, if you check in the library, next to the table under the window, you'll find my grandfather's telescope and my father's microscope… How strange, think about it, my father studied lives up close with a microscope, my grandfather searched for other distant lives with his telescope, and both of them used lenses. But you discover life with the naked eye, not from a distance, not too close, just at eye level… My father loved New York so much, and he died before he got there… I wanted to see New York, too, but I never did, it never worked out. Have you been there, to New York? – what am I saying – in your world, who hasn't been to New York… You know, I'd really love to take that plane I was telling you about, one of these nights, maybe so, maybe so… Sorry, what was I saying? – I'm all over the place – maybe I was sleeping, you start talking nonsense when you're nodding off, maybe we'll pick this up later, it seems late now… You think I could have a smoke, just two puffs, and maybe Frau wouldn't notice? At least open the shutters – it's so damned hot.

Word is, you've never wanted to go on pippopippi. I'm glad, good for you, it's always so full of windbags who are on there just to show off how much they know, what everybody likes this year, if that government official's a good dresser or bad, if it would be better to vote a little this way or that, what's going to happen with that hole in the ozone, or what if the world were square, you never know… who knows how many times you were invited on, especially after that prize you won in the States for your novel, that's typical: they won't even look at you, but win something in the States, and you're a star, and there's no escaping pippopippi… in your novel, you really make Tristano out to be a hero, but he's afraid, too, and this I liked, heroes are afraid, the simpletons might not know that, but he overcomes his fear… there's another twist, though – and here you've done something really clever – because maybe he's managed to overcome his fear because his fear is overpowering?…

in short, the hero overcomes fear because fear overcomes him. You didn't quite get it right, but the idea's intriguing... You're a complicated guy – no one writes a book like that and lets pippopippi get the better of him... you're also something of a senator – excuse me for that – what I mean is, you have this severe manner about you that you've done a good job of cultivating; when I imagined you, it was always in a white toga, like some Roman senator, a bit like Seneca, if I may, also considering your writing style, but maybe Seneca wasn't a senator, I'm not sure... But listen, isn't not going on pippopippi like going on, anyway? Sorry to be tricky here, but this way, everyone's talking about your refusing to go on pippopippi, you're on everybody's lips, so in the end, not going on is like you went on... because pippopippi's horrific, my dear writer, go on, don't go on, either way, you're fucked – that ever occur to you? I heard what they said about you on that pippopippi show Frau likes to call Tube Flush. I'm extremely informed about that thing over there even if I don't watch it, Frau keeps me posted. Last month, when I was first bedridden, she shows up at the door and says, young sir, tonight on Tube Flush they talked about that writer you were reading yesterday. Get to the point, Renate, I say. Well, today's program was, Having the Courage to Change Your Mind, and the host introduces his guests and says in his syrupy voice, we also invited a famous author on who wrote a prize-winning novel about courage, but unfortunately he declined our invitation, we can only hope he wasn't too frightened to be on our program, oh famous writer... we're waiting for you... see how nice we are? – let's be brave now… Okay, Renate, I get it, and – ? Well, aren't you the one who said you needed someone to come listen to you and that he had to be a writer? But before I could answer, she shut the door again…

I feel good today, really good, and I'm going to tell you the whole thing, word for word, logically, it's the set piece, in your book, it'll be the set piece, listen and write, write and be quiet – ready?… It's dawn. Tristano is alone in the goddamned woods, and he's afraid. Because even heroes are afraid, you said so yourself. Besides, Tristano doesn't know he's a hero yet, he's alone, hiding behind a boulder near the commander's shelter, he knows he's alone because all his comrades went down to the valley that night, under orders by that same commander, to attack a barracks, there were weapons, ammunition in the village, fascists standing guard, they had to go on a sortie, so his comrades went down to the valley, and Tristano's alone on that goddamned dawn in the goddamned woods, on a dawn that should be pink and pale blue, soft, a dawn not made for days of tragedy but for loving, for holding onto a woman in bed, for love, not crouching behind a rock and trembling with fear; it's an icy dawn. How many of them? They're usually so cautious, there are never just a few when they make their raids, there could be ten, twenty, a whole platoon. Tristano heard shots, heard *Maschinenpistolen* fire, screaming, and now grave silence, the sun rising on that dawn, a dangerous dawn, because for Tristano, daylight's the enemy, he's alone behind that rock, and there are so many of them. After the slaughter, silence. But what are they waiting for? Why aren't they leaving? What are they doing in there? Maybe looking for charts, maps, notes. They'd done it: in one master stroke, they'd eliminated the most dangerous commander of all, a great commander, not just any commander, that one, not some eager spur-of-the-moment partisan, no, an old soldier, in the Great War, already an officer in fifteen, with enormous responsibilities, a man who knows strategy, who's calm, skilled, careful, strong-willed, he scares the Nazis, he's caused many casualties, the order came down from the German High Command in Italy to eliminate him, the men under him don't matter, he's the one, crush the rebel head, the body goes too, just poor bastards on the run without a plan, it's urgent to carry this out, and now they have. But someone led them there, otherwise how'd they find the shelter? Tristano knows this space, it's also the headquarters, there are four rooms in that abandoned farmhouse, a kitchen on the main floor, where they meet, discuss their military actions, develop their plans, get their orders, and the adjoining room is where two soldiers from the Savoy Army sleep, two young soldiers, two sweet, inexperienced boys who are better off not seeing any action, who serve as sentries, the commander's bodyguards; upstairs is a hayloft, where the peasants dry figs and chestnuts on straw mats, and then a room where the commander sleeps. The gunfire was downstairs. Tristano saw the flashes through the windows on either side of the sagging wooden door of that fairy-tale cottage at the edge of the woods. But why aren't they coming out? It's cold. It's a cold dawn. Behind that rock, Tristano is afraid. Heroes aren't afraid, but Tristano doesn't know he's a hero yet, he's just a man, alone, clutching the submachine gun of a dead German, his hands frozen, his feet frozen, he can't seem to think straight though his mind is racing, he keeps staring at that sagging door, now and then he looks around, barely glances, and doesn't see a thing, all he knows is it's growing lighter, soon it will be day. He thinks: how long since I heard the shots? – ten minutes – an hour? He'd slept in the shed near the woods where the peasants kept their pigs, he decided to sleep there that night instead of in the cave down by the stream where he usually slept with his comrades. Why? He can't say why. Why, why, why…

…because, because, because. You came here to find out the answers to Tristano's life. But there are no answers to life, didn't anybody tell you?… why write? Or are you one of those, the kind looking for answers, wanting to put everything in its place?… Okay, listen, one answer, one because, is that he'd met the American girl in the mountains, I already brought her up, this Marilyn that he immediately started calling Rosamunda, and sometimes just Guagliona, but not too often, when he gathered her hair at her neck, her hair that she wore in a braid during the day, and he'd say undo your braid, Mary Magdalene, undo your braid, Guagliona… You want answers to other whys, why he wound up in the mountains, and how, and when, and Daphne, whatever became of her… You're far too curious, writer – what do you care? Besides, listen, it made sense, what else could he do, he was a drifter by then, a deserter, he'd returned home after Badoglio sent everyone home, and he had to decide if he would hide under the straw in the barn with the Germans raking or go find his king in Brindisi or somewhere around there… He didn't like the idea of hiding under the straw – would you? – if you were him, would you want to go join a king who'd left the Italians to rot while he went off and ate orecchiette with turnip tops?… But in a way, Tristano did the same thing by going off to fight in the Resistance in the mountains, because the turnip heads came along after… but that's all in hindsight, if you could call it sight because I've had my morphine… Did you know Frau gave me two doses? She's like that: one day stingy, the next day giving me a double-dose, she gets emotional… she's annoying, you've seen that tough mug on her, but inside… you ask me, she's always crying on the inside instead of the outside, I don't know how she does it, if it's just her or because she's German, sometimes the Germans do seem like they might be people crying on the inside instead of the outside, just read some of what they've written… we're different, we seem to be sobbing on the outside but inside nothing's changed… a matter of hydraulics… you ask me, even the soul obeys the laws of hydraulics… I'm lost, where was I?… you'd like to know about Daphne, the whys and wherefores to his leaving her in Greece… patience, now, was he supposed to take her into the mountains, with everything she'd suffered in her own country?… and what do you care about Daphne anyway?

Daphne's the one beautiful thing in this whole damned story, the rest of it's a mess... you don't believe me? – look around, then, if you don't believe me, and ask yourself why – no, ask yourself what good it was, what point there was to Tristano's heading into the mountains with a telescope on his shoulder... ah, you didn't know that, did you, that's not something you'd ever think of, and I'm glad I'm telling you, you writers love this sort of thing, then you can start to embellish... up in the mountains, Tristano carried a submachine gun, sure, and he became the hero you know with that submachine gun, but up till then he carried a brass telescope he was fond of, that belonged to his grandfather; as a boy, he discovered the sky with that thing, and he brought it along to see the stars from mountain tops, because the higher up you are the better you see the stars... An Englishman who wrote books like you said we are all in the gutter but some of us are looking at the stars, and maybe Tristano wanted to see the stars because his country was truly down in the gutter... And your country? – how do you like it now?

I just remembered a little more of Frau's poem, a very long poem, she recites it bit by bit, and it's torture... I saw a toad leap from the ditch and carry away my truest love; this smooth, loathsome creature, soft and velvety pale, stole an old locket and brought it back again, corroded with spit, an old locket, a picture inside, her sleeping echo.

…The cicadas have stopped… it must be dark out, maybe you're tired of writing. But isn't this why you came? I'm tired of talking, too, but this is why I sent for you; if Frau comes in and disturbs us, tell her we'll go on for a little yet, just ten more minutes, because I'm not so sure tomorrow I'll have the strength to go on. And it's important, you know this better than me, you reconstructed this in your book, you even won a prize, am I right? If I send you away now you might have trouble sleeping tonight, might sleep worse than me, worrying I might lose hold of the thread, and that you'll be screwed, right? – that you'll have traveled all this way to listen to me in the stink of carbolic acid, of gangrene, and right at the best part, I'll lose the thread… don't worry, I haven't lost it, because that sagging door is swinging open, and the house is dark, and Tristano can't see a thing. Out, he thinks, out, you monsters. And there's one, finally. But he looks familiar – it's Stefano, who was always so friendly, the school janitor down in the village, who'd made it clear he could be trusted. And now he's dressed in black, a tassel on his fez – the pig. Stefano looks around, cautious, checking no one's there to see him, he signals toward the house, out comes a German, then two, three, four… Fire, Tristano tells himself, it's just four assholes. He presses down on the trigger, impatient, but, no, hold back – any more inside, he's fucked. And now the others are advancing toward him through the meadow, coming closer, if they see him he's a dead man – what now – it's a poker hand, this waiting, throw down your cards, Tristano, fire. And then he hears a woman's voice, singing, a lovely voice singing a slow melody, strange, strange words, an old lullaby, old like that voice is old – but how can a woman be singing up here in the woods, the dawn after a slaughter? And is that voice even real? Tristano listens, and he remembers what the church fathers wrote, that it's an internal voice, that it can't come from outside of him, and he alone hears it, and these are the voices of the angels, the church fathers said, and the only ones who hear them are those that can hear them or want to hear what they long to hear; it's an old woman's voice, an enchanting voice singing… I had a pony all dappled gray, that counted clip-clops to the moon, I had a dark-haired boy who went away, oh love and I are out of tune… and he knows it's a cradle song, and then the meadow, the mountains, the woods, everything begins to sway, as though an unseen hand, a woman's hand, is rocking a cradle, and there's only that voice singing, I had a pony without a tail, I tied that pony on a rope, and on that rope it used to pull, like a man in love and full of hope… and everything is swaying in front of him, and now all the Germans are finally out in the open, gathered together, caught, enraptured by this woman's voice that's rocking the whole countryside to sleep, it's beddy-bye, now beddy-bye, you're nonna's little baby… so sings the siren's voice, casting its spell over the Germans, who are almost asleep, lost to oblivion, frozen, side by side, like a family photo, a monument to the dead. Tristano fires his first volley, a second, a third, he's firing and singing along with that voice that's saved him, it's beddy-bye, now beddy-bye, you're nonna's little baby, oh… the woods echo with machine-gun fire, clusters of echoes bouncing off the hillsides, from mountain to valley, then fading into the distance, like rolling thunder. Now Tristano is the new commander of the partisan brigade, the mantle of the old commander killed by the Germans has passed to him, though he doesn't know it yet, he doesn't know anything, Tristano, as he stands there, in the open, out past the rock he hid behind, stands there, lit by the rising sun, which seems fitting, how heroes appear in the movies. Go on, Tristano, approach your fallen prey, set your foot on a German's chest and raise your machine gun high in triumph, that's how we want to remember you, these are your memories, we're writing your life. And now you can go, writer, it must be late, enough for today, you've heard what you wanted to hear.

Life isn't arranged in alphabetical order like all of you believe. It seems… a little here, a little there, sprinkled as you will, granules, the problem's gathering them up later, a pile of sand, and which granule supports the next? Sometimes what's on top, what seems supported by everything else, is really holding everything in place, because that sand pile doesn't obey the laws of physics, take away a granule you didn't think held up anything else, and the whole pile collapses, sliding, spreading out, and all you're left to do is trace in the sand with your finger, making squiggle marks, comings and goings, paths leading nowhere, and you go on and on this way, tracing back and forth, but where did that damn grain of sand get to that held everything in place… and then one day your finger stops all on its own, and can't go on with its squiggling, and there's a strange outline in the sand, a drawing that's meaningless, absurd, and you have the sneaking suspicion the meaning of this whole business was just in the squiggling.

…Correction: that dream I told you, the one on the beach, that wasn't Rosamunda after all, it was Daphne… now that I think about it, Tristano went into that wooden bathing hut with his Daphne, I promise this is true, I can prove it, I didn't think of it before, the watermelon… In that hut, there's a watermelon split in half, a beautiful red watermelon sitting on the wooden shelf where they kept their bathing suits, I see it like it's now, along the road to the beach there was this little man with a little fruit stand selling peaches, melons, and *karpùzhi*, the word's come back to me now, and Daphne adored *karpùzhi*, *karpùzhi* meant Greece to her, there's even watermelon ice cream in Greece, you know, I remember one summer in Crete – the first time I went with her – and an enormous, white beach, and the watermelon the man kept buried in crushed ice on his little rolling fruit stand, along the road to the beach… and certain afternoons, on that beach… in the bathing hut, making love with his Daphne, after chasing each other into the water, and licking all the salt off each other… and then they'd eat a slice of watermelon… it couldn't have been Rosamunda, Marilyn didn't like watermelon, Americans don't like watermelon, maybe because they're all water and no vitamins.

I heard what Frau whispered to you… sir, don't write down what he tells you under morphine. Don't you listen to her: you write everything down, everything, morphine or no morphine, gather everything you possibly can, the pieces blown to smithereens, down to the last granule, my delirium is also me…

…Are you familiar with a poem about a mother dressed in black crying over the body of her son killed in the square? Frau read it to me this morning. Frau has the gift of prophecy, she's ahead of me, she's always reading me a poem that refers to something I want to tell you, today she came into my bedroom and read this one, and it's not Sunday, this I'm sure of, and I started thinking that the story I'm telling you, that maybe you think makes no sense, is like a musical score where every now and then an instrument will start talking on its own, in its own voice, and there's a baton directing all that music, only you can't see the conductor, but you know who's holding that baton? – I think it's Frau.

…You have no idea how quickly an August can end, hurling itself against early September, like a car ramming a tree, crumpling, deflated like an accordion out of breath. Such arrogance, those days of summer, during the Feast of the Assumption

59

or when the sky's lit up with fireworks on the night of San Lorenzo and the senses seem so full and life, a cavern from the vaults of heaven, but then four rain drops, the coriander's gone to seed, and in a single day that bloated, bombastic month is swallowed up... Life's that way, too, like August, you start to realize there's a lapse between what's said and done, when you really weren't expecting this, the elastic's worn out, can't be stretched, and the raven shows up in the corner to croak its *nevermore*... The house, empty as a dried gourd, and he emptier still, and the dead seasons, and the current day dead as a doornail, everything was conspiring for a completely ataraxic state, the stillness of the horizon, only a few lisped words, directed at nothing, unheard. And that thick fog... How do you feel? Doctor Ziegler asked him. Shooshoo, Tristano answered, I feel shooshoo, as to the rest, I'd be fine if I weren't feeling so shooshoo. Doctor Ziegler didn't understand; he asked Tristano to please explain, *bitte, Herr Tristano, bitte*. Shooshoo's like rain-soaked cabbage, Doctor, have you ever seen cabbage with its limp outer leaves in the mud? They're shooshoo... And then he added, it's like I've seen a tranglumanglo, you understand? Doctor Ziegler began to suspect this was some sort of language of the unconscious, but reluctantly, as he wasn't of that school... but what on earth did these words mean? Tristano hesitated, secretive. Well, they come to me at night – no – they think of me – really – I'm thought up, they're the ones that think of me, they nip at me – no – it's more like they sting me, tiny slivers of something, tiny letters, exploding into a thousand pieces, and they arrive like they're washing in on the evening tide… Doctor Ziegler had his hands behind his back, his chin on his chest. So, they're dreams? he asked. No answer. Half-dreams, then? Yes, that's it, Doctor, almost – no, not really – more like memories, floating in their own sea foam, I'm on the edge of sleep, a few reach me, sting me, others, all I have to do is dangle my arm alongside the bed to fish some up. Doctor Ziegler kept pacing back and forth as though he wanted to dig a rut in the floor, he didn't care that Tristano was slouched in his chair on the porch, it was as if he'd found him in his sleepless bed. Try fishing one up now, he said, just let yourself go, let your arm hang over the edge, close your eyes, pretend I'm not here… Silence. Doctor Ziegler froze, held his breath. All you could hear was the countryside's breathing, the ground, the smell of stubble in the valley, the buzzing blue flies, a bee, a barking dog, but far far away, another world. I caught a can of gambusinen, but it's open, the key's turning up the rusty lid, Tristano mumbled as if in a trance, *nichts, absolut nichts, gambusinen kaputt*. Doctor Ziegler was worrying his hands behind his back. Gambusinen? – *was bedeutet gambusinen*, go on, Herr Tristano, concentrate. Oh… oh… oh… Tristano was searching for something, or perhaps those concentric rings of sound rising in his throat meant he was already lost to a world of dreams? Ziegler waited patiently, silently. I should talk about old schnabelewopskian customs, Tristano mumbled, ancient anthropology, Doctor, practically geology, and he was in full flight now over a truly incomprehensible land not to be found on any maps, probably tied to the archipelago of his imagination, and over there was Utopia Island. Schnabelewops was a principality, a swatch of land high in the mountains, with a view of the sea, and that sea was the Greek sea, where Venus was virgin-born, it was understood, a country of impervious peaks but also soft slopes and meadows and olive and chestnut trees and crisscrossed by countless streams, their water as clean, as crystal-clear as the water where Orlando christened his sword Durlindana or Dionigi di Gaula bathed his feet after his long, long march, as the mad hidalgo tells it. And during the local wheat festivals or on the many scorching-hot days, the people would joyfully splash about in these streams, to the shrieks of young ladies. And there were so many streams, the Schnabelewopskians hadn't even tried counting them for their maps. What was the point? Each village had a stream running beside it or even dividing it in two, so that there were great cultural divides going back a thousand years between those villagers on the right bank or the left, and a Nordic folklorist, who'd wandered everywhere collecting ancient songs, had recorded some ancient treasures where the maid who'd left to marry sang with longing for the land of her fathers that she'd abandoned when she wed and crossed over the stream to live in the house facing her own that was in a whole other country; and wading in, she soaked her stockings... With this last effort, Tristano grew quiet, eyes closed, his hand gone fishing, dangling off the lounge chair. Not asleep though... Doctor Ziegler was afraid to interrupt his oneiric space, which was sacred to every patient and crucial to every therapist. The countryside was slowly breathing in and out. It was midday.

Doctor Ziegler should have been in his office in town, but of course he'd cancelled all his appointments: this patient was too interesting. Tristano started to speak again, but perhaps he was truly sailing in his oneiric space now, talking about gambusinen, aquatic creatures presumably from his childhood, no doubt part of a fantastic zoology known only to the disturbed or to poets who'd never written any poetry, creatures which, if you listened to his semi-garbled words, seemed to fall somewhere between crustaceans and proper fish, meaning, with gills and fins. Antidiluvian creatures, Doctor Ziegler thought, from the earliest of times, when everything was just coming into being, when taxonomy wasn't yet possible, and you couldn't distinguish flower from fruit, fish from fowl, insect from mammal… You see, Doctor, sir, I'm not sure I can explain: a tiny creature like a freshwater crawfish, pink-colored, but with no keratin shell, so, soft like a dormouse, with a tiny round head that's sprouting four miniature tentacles, maybe a centimeter and a half, two centimeters long, nothing more, and extremely tender, it feeds off something like the moss that grows in the cleanest streams in the principality, the gambusinen gorge on it, an exquisite green, like nothing else, and it lingers in their meat, like a truffle cutting the slight bitterness of porcini mushrooms… Doctor Ziegler listened and was silent. The cicadas were raging, and heat settled over the pergola. It was August… It was an August like this one, writer, and Tristano didn't need any morphine to step outside himself, he was out of his mind all on his own. I wanted to tell you about this later, but it's come to me now and so I told you now, be patient, I'm sure it won't make sense in your book, let it go… Listen, it must be nearly evening and Frau's coming to give me my morphine, but I don't want it tonight. I'm hungry, tell her I'm hungry, that I want a cup of broth, a cup of chicken broth, there was a time I'd ask for gambusinen, but now they're extinct, all that's left of them are empty tins with the key turning up the rusty lid… Tell Frau that since there aren't any gambusinen, I'll make do with a cup of chicken broth – you'll see – she'll know.


Ferruccio said you writers always see yourselves in light of the future, as posthumous, and I thought about what you set in motion by telling my story in the first person, as if you were Tristano… you'd already consigned me to the future, like a tombstone, and you saw your own reflection there, because that tombstone reflected your own image back to you, like you thought you'd be for posterity… But I'm changing that image right under your nose, no, it's more topsy-turvy, face down feet up, like a carnival mirror… I feel sorry for you, but I'm not sure what you were expecting when you came here to see me, I'm not here to confirm anything, just the opposite… never trust mirrors, right then and there they seem to show your image, but they really distort it, or even worse, they absorb your image, drink up everything, suck you in as well… Mirrors are porous, writer, and you didn't even know.

He didn't answer, Marios, staring off at nothing, his finger stirring the coffee grinds at the bottom of his glass, he looked like a failed fortuneteller searching for an answer that couldn't be found, and he just kept quiet… The same small Plaka square, one cold sunny day, the impassive Acropolis above… Marios, it's me, I'm back, please, look at me. And then Marios spoke, his voice neutral, like a doctor handing out a diagnosis or a judge a sentence… the mountains are the same, and the stones, and the trees, but everything's finished, there's no one left, they're all dead, I'm dead, too; Field Marshal Papagos, that black-hearted leader, gave Greece a new Duce and a new king, identical to the ones that came before, the British lent a hand, the Americans, too, General Skolby, the great strategist, expert at mass shootings… the British and their younger cousins have two democracies, the good kind, for internal use, and then the damaged kind, left to molder in the storehouses of time, the export kind, suitable for poor people, so poor they'll swallow anything… and now you're back, Tristano, I see that you're back, and you're asking about your comrades, about Daphne… your comrades are dead, Daphne's far away, I don't know where, giving her concerts, it's not as though Greece needs her music, the marshals want patriotic music for the people in their new Greece… I see that you're back, you're back like you promised, but maybe you didn't notice ten years have gone by, you left in forty-three – when the beast in my country is dead I'll be back, you said – I think the beast has been dead in your country for quite some time, but here he's alive and well, like I told you, if you're feeling nostalgic for the Peloponnese Mountains, go up there for a stroll, go and clear your lungs… Tristano, go back where you came from, to your own country, if you came for us, you're awfully late, if it was for Daphne, come back next year, or maybe in a couple of years… Writer, if you'd known about this, you'd have told the story like you know how: the hero who arranges a time to return and then shows up ten years too late warrants a few pages, a parody of Ulysses, a joke of a Ulysses who got on the wrong tram, the one for Pancuervo instead of Ithaca… I don't know how your protagonist would have answered Marios if you'd written what I told you, what excuse would your Tristano have come up with? Sorry if I'm jumping to conclusions here, I'm only guessing… I can see a solemn Tristano, with wounded pride… I received the War Cross, he says in a grave voice, I'm a hero, Marios, you have to understand how many obligations fill a hero's days, the staged appearances, diplomatic missions, ambassadorships for peace and brotherhood, ceremonies, conferences… and a man like Marios, who'd fought for freedom, even though it turned out badly, would understand and embrace him. But Tristano gave another excuse entirely… I didn't come before because of one small detail, he said with conviction, one damned detail. Just like that, a ridiculous excuse, it smacks of comedy, someone getting on the wrong tram… and if you write Tristano's life, this is the truth, the whole truth, and nothing but the truth, so help me… But listen, writer, if you want to write this according to your own ideas, how you might have if you'd known about this earlier, then feel free. Your choice – and who'd object?

God is in the details, a Jewish scholar said, a philologist, I think. But so's the Devil. It was a summer day, blue, Tristano remembers, even the city he remembers as blue, though it was actually a rose-colored city, with pink and yellow buildings all along the moats and ancient walls by the sea. The buildings crowded along the bulwarks had sheets hanging out the windows to dry, like white flags, and they were snapping that day in the northwest wind. And Tristano, when he'd go see Taddeo, rode his red motorcycle, because he liked riding his motorcycle along the coast, the road just outside the city sloped down, winding sharply around rocky cliffs where tamarisk and prickly pear grew, and from there you could enjoy the vast panorama, the sky-blue sea, with sailboats on the horizon, and after a few curves, Taddeo's pensione came into view. Not a real pensione, though; it was called Taddeo Zimmer, a low structure that Taddeo had put up with his own two hands, right below the cliffs, by a short, pebble beach. Eight small rooms with a kitchenette and bath, each with its own terrace divided from the others by privet shrubs in terracotta pots, to give the Germans – the Krauts, Taddeo called them – a sense of being in the Mediterranean, as he liked to say. He'd become a great friend of the krauts, and they were devoted clients, because Taddeo's pensione was modest and his customers were mainly workers from the Ruhr Valley, and at night they'd sit with Taddeo and play cards. Taddeo had killed many Germans. He counted his kills in a filthy notebook, in German, jotting down the hour and place, *ein, zwei, drei, vier, fünf, sechs, sieben*, and next to those he'd killed with the highest military rank, he put three small stars like in the Michelin Guide. Taddeo and Tristano first met a few years before in those mountains behind them. Taddeo was a small wild boy who lived in the woods with his family of foresters, exterminated by the SS that the Republicans had guided into the woods. Hidden in the oak trees in front of their house, he'd witnessed their murder from a distance, through tortured, wild eyes, while he stood among the branches. But during the retreat, one of the Nazis left his squad to find a fresh egg in the chicken coop; Taddeo waited behind a holm-oak, and when the soldier went by, smashed his face in with a knotty branch. Then he took the soldier's *Maschinenpistole* and climbed the slopes to join the partisans. By now, they didn't have much to say to each other, he and Taddeo. The reality was he went to Taddeo's because he enjoyed riding his motorcycle along that steep road to the sea, a road filled with wind and different scents… And now we've come to the detail. Instead of going by motorcycle that day, Tristano went by bus. Why? I couldn't say. In the piazza that stretched out behind the moats, between the Mussolini-era post office and the first piers of the port, there was a small market of fresh-caught fish. Tristano was wandering by the fish still flopping in crates when he suddenly felt the urge to see Taddeo, the bus stop was nearby – it was just like that. He bought the proper fish for Taddeo to make his spicy *cacciucco* stew, he crossed the road, it was almost noon, only ten minutes to wait. Tristano remembers two precise

sounds, as if he were hearing them now, the noon bells ringing and the bus honking its horn, announcing its arrival, right
on schedule. And then a voice murmured in his ear: Glenn
Miller's more cheerful than Schubert. Tristano swung round,
and all he could manage to say was, what are you doing here,
where'd you come from, why aren't you back in America? I've
been waiting for you, Rosamunda answered… I'm not making
this up, writer, that's exactly what she said, I've been waiting
for you, which is a crazy answer, because none of this made any
sense, and then she added, I'm coming with you – we have to
talk. But then during the trip they didn't exchange a word, they
got off at the second stop, took the road to the small town by
the shore, and reached Taddeo's pensione. Tristano handed the
fish over to the girl who did all the general maid work, because
Taddeo wasn't back yet. Marilyn asked Tristano if they could
get a room. The *Zimmer*, like all the other *Zimmer*, was a room
with plaster walls that were whitewashed and textured for a
Mediterranean effect, and prints of old photographs were hanging, fishermen in rolled-up trousers who sat mending fish pots.
A small door led to the bathroom, a closet-sized room with a
toilet, sink, and showerhead fixed to the wall with a plastic curtain to pull around it. The sliding glass door led onto the terrace sheltered by privet shrubs, Tristano stepped out and lit a
cigarette. They hadn't spoken a word yet. Marilyn tiptoed over
to him and draped her arms around his shoulders. What do you
want? he asked. You, she said. Tristano turned and grabbed her
wrists. Rosamunda, he said, this is ridiculous, you can't pretend

nothing happened, things ended badly between us, let's not make it any worse. There was a green park bench against the low terrace wall. Marilyn sat down and crossed her legs. None of that matters anymore, Clark, she said, I swear, none of that matters. But I don't love you anymore – and don't call me Clark – actually, Tristano said, I never loved you. Me neither, Marilyn said, but what the body wants is something else, and it's the same for you, I know it is, I know because I remember. Forget it, Tristano said, try a little harder, you're good at forgetting. They had their dinner on the covered veranda that Taddeo used as a restaurant. Hardly anyone was out there, it wasn't high season yet. Taddeo served them in silence, as if they were any two customers. They didn't talk, either, they were listening to the waves lapping against the pebbles on the shore. It was nearly dawn before he broke the silence. I have to go to Greece, he said, there's a woman waiting for me, I'm in love with her. Marilyn stroked his chest and whispered, if she's waited this long, she can wait a little longer, and she hugged him tightly, first, come with me, I have to go to Spain, come with me, I was lying before: I'm in love with you. In the frame of the window, a light went by in the distance, probably a fishing boat. Maybe I am, too, Tristano said, my body is, anyway, but for now, let me sleep, I'm tired.

…Do me a favor, call Frau for me, I need my injection, if she says she already gave me one, then you do it… you should do something besides just taking down my dictation, do something concrete to earn this story, so you'll be telling it, so you'll become the author… but do me a favor now, call Frau for me, I need my injection, I'm afraid I'll start complaining, and heroes can't complain, they just turn to the gods, or drop dead without a word, just strike them in the heel, me, I don't have any gods, and my heel's up to my balls, I'm slowly being devoured, you've seen it… Hurry up, call Frau for me, and then I'll tell you something in the style of old Ernest, that old bastard Ernest, who saw so much in life before pointing a double-barrel shotgun at his heart, I'm sure you'll like my story, it makes sense, writer, because you like literature, call Frau for me…


You're like Pinocchio with a belly ache, Tristano said and imitated her: hii-ick. Marilyn hiccupped twice, you're awful, she said, it's true, I had my own paradoxical affair: my heart was so full of this frustrated love for you, there was very little room for a man in my life, and that paradoxical situation was, paradoxically, the only one that worked for me, Clark. Don't call me that, Tristano answered, I already told you, I'm not Clark anymore, I'm Tristano now, and I don't understand the comparison you're making, Guagliona, but the fact is, Cary fucked you again and again and I can't, and maybe that's what love is to you, Guagliona, you've traded the clapper for the bell, and now what is it you want from me – a child? – it's getting late, you're longing to desire something, but time in life isn't in step with the time of desire, a hundred years can go by in a single day, so look for someone else, the time for Tristano has up and gone.

…I think I promised you an episode in the style of old Ernest, I'm not sure if you like his writing, but I should tell you about Pancuervo first. You'll want to know what that is. It's a remote place in Spain where the rain stays mainly in the plain. And no one goes there. But Tristano's life crossed paths with Pancuervo…

…who knows when it'll go by, the girl said, here in Spain they drop the crossing bar as if the train's arriving in five minutes, though it might not get there till tomorrow, that's how this country works. There should be a train for Pancuervo, the man said, but maybe there aren't more trains for Pancuervo, kaput, and maybe Pancuervo doesn't exist, it's a place you invented… The sun was ruthless, but inside the small café, the air was still tolerable. The curtain of beer bottle corks rippled in the warm breeze and produced a sound like Asian music. They ordered something to drink, the owner was a small, pot-bellied man with a mustache like a sad eyebrow. Strange, he said, that man has a barber's mustache but owns a café, his mustache is all wrong. Why? the girl asked, he needs a specific kind of mustache? He sipped his beer, sure, he said, take a look at people's features here, it's a lesson in anthropology; in my diary, I've drawn a series of mustaches in various categories; there's a whole world of mustaches in this country, take the Civil Guard: they've got this kind. He drew a mark on his napkin. Lawyers have this kind instead. Another mark. Judges have this kind, almost like lawyers, but not quite. University professors have this kind if they support the regime and this kind if they don't. Landowners have this kind, and this is the mustache of the great Spanish landowner who backs the Generalissimo. Whose own mustache is like so, practically like the others, but only the Generalissimo wears this kind, so you recognize it right off… if you really think about the story of our century, it's a story of mustaches, the German's little clipped mustache, the Russian's big peasant mustache… Il Duce was hairless altogether, like we Italians are, we're only hairy in our souls, like me, but you have no idea, my girl, you think you're hairier than I am, and you're a hill without a blade of grass. I'd like you to grow a mustache, the girl said, at your age, it would suit you. The man smiled. So I'd look more like Clark Gable, he said, sorry, but I'm not a movie star, and I'm not your partisan comrade anymore, and stop calling me Clark – got it? He signaled the café owner who was nodding off behind the bar. *Dos más*, he said, pointing to a bottle of beer. Anyway, I had a hunch I'd see you again, the girl said, that I'd see you one summer night, like I predicted in my letter. What letter? he asked, I never got any letter. The girl had a vague, lost air about her, as though she were watching the flies buzzing around.

My letter didn't include that June night, when you brought me to the pensione, she said, we didn't really come together at the pensione. But I did fuck you all night, the man said, so plenty of coming together. You're so crass, she said. And lucky for us, you're very refined, the man said, and your point? That tonight, we've really come together, the girl said, but men will never understand, you men don't understand these things. We don't get metaphysics, the man said. And he started laughing quietly, trying not to. Clark, please, she said. Don't call me Clark, he said, I'm not Clark anymore, I told you already, I'm Tristano, that's what I want, my name's Tristano now. Tristano's so fake, the girl answered, so artificial, I don't like it, it's someone else's name, maybe your brother, you always told me you had a brother and you never told me his name, maybe it's your brother. The man smiled and started squiggling on his wet beer glass with his finger. Now you get it, he said, I'm my brother. She tried to take his hand, but he pulled away: he wanted to draw on his glass. Tristano, she said, yesterday you told me there are all different ways and levels of falling in love, and we'd feel less guilty if each of us took half the blame. He swore. Stop being so crass, she said, it doesn't suit you; you know, Cary never tried to hold on to me, he loved me, or rather, he wanted what was best for me, or what I thought was best for me, he grew so terribly sad, but you see everyone as plotting against you, and you take your revenge in your own way, and always up the ante. The man dug in his pocket and pulled out a piece of paper. He read to her: because Cary never tried to hold on to me or see me again, he loved me, or rather, he wanted what was best for me, or what I thought was best for me… he grew so terribly sad, and I was the cause of that pain, understand? He looked at her. Excuse me, my dear, he said, but you're repeating yourself, they're the same exact words from this letter, we're in Spain, the crossing bar is down, the train might never come and the schedule's off, and you, off-schedule, are repeating some loudspeaker warning about a canceled train – why? Because Cary was unhappy, she said, and I was really in love, that's why: for me, it was like finding a home at last, and one night he phoned me, he said, please come, I need you, for me, it was like finding a home, I'm a poor drifter, American, an East-coast girl from a lower middle-class family, with a notary for a father and an idiot for a mother, you wouldn't understand, Clark. Don't call me Clark, the man said, and cut the bullshit – your father's Sicilian and emigrated to Brooklyn, and the Americans took him with them when they landed in Sicily because he could provide contacts with the right godfathers – you know what I'm talking about – they sent you both on missions, you each had your specific duties, and as for Cary, well, I don't know, he's a sinister character, but that's your business, it's your life. He was the one freedom I allowed myself, the girl said, and you only live once. The owner came to clean the table and flicked the flies away with his rag. The train left, he said, it arrived and left again, perhaps you two didn't realize, it was the train for Pancuervo. Freedom's a supple word, the man said, you know, Guagliona, I keep asking myself if it's the same word when I use it, maybe so, but a word in one person's mouth is different in the mouth of another. The girl checked her watch. Clark, she said, what freedoms are you defending? The man looked out the window. The landscape was bleak, the hills were like white elephants. Let's do an already-been-there, he said, you're not the one who has to have an abortion, not to mention, my seed's never taken hold – and it's late besides – I'm the one who has to have an abortion, you know, I'm starting to think I was confused over the freedom I defended, and I've come with you to understand it better, why you're trying to pull me into this ugly business, you're all pretty simple, but that doesn't make you any less dangerous, you're all so simple you think if someone didn't support communism, then Francisco Franco's fine, and I really want to understand what your Marshall Plan consists of, if this is what it's about. It does benefit me, person-ally, Marilyn said, I found a do-gooder, his seed's taken hold, and I have no intention of getting an abortion – sorry to change the ending to your little story alla Hemingway. More bullshit, I'm sure, Tristano said, you've gone round the bend. He slapped some coins on the table. Maybe I'll go home, he said, I'm not enjoying this little charade. She took his hand. You never get it, she said, it's like you close your eyes at all the important parts – it's true – it's bullshit – but I need you, I need you to protect me, please, Tristano, I need you to protect me.

Tristano, Guagliona said, what are you doing, tell me; she was staring off to the sea that reflected in her eyes. Tristano spread wide his arms to embrace the horizon. I should defend freedom, he told her, the freedom I've gone looking for, and that I hold dear, but the truth is I'm not sure what freedom is anymore, now I've been dragged into something that doesn't concern me – I don't know – when we were in the mountains it was all so clear, or it seemed that way at least, and now nothing's clear, and I'd like to understand… Sorry, a little aside: you should tell Frau I don't want any morphine right now, but I need some ergotamine, I have a splitting headache, or maybe I'm just afraid I'll get one, it's probably on the dresser, see if you can find it, a bottle of pills… If I had to say where the conversation I was discussing took place, and especially, when it took place, that would be a real problem, writer. But that's your fault, too – you never help me out at all – you don't utter a word, never ask me anything, true, you're following the orders I gave you when I called: not a peep out of you, I said, come, write, and not a peep out of you… but now you're being too obedient, if I drop the thread, then come up behind me, the years are piling up, places, too; sometimes, all I need from you is a quick observation, a question to help steer me straight… help me out… I think you're doing it on purpose, out of spite, you're spiteful, too, in your own way; you said to yourself: this old bag of bones is so arrogant, thinks it's a privilege for me to write his life, and treats me like a goddamned idiot, all right, let's see if he'll give up finally and ask for help, ask me to lend a hand, shed some light on things, help him unravel some of his memories… that's what you thought, right?, and now you're waiting for me to start groveling … please… please, you know the basic outlines of my life, what I mean by this is where I was in forty-nine or fifty-four or sixty-seven or sixty-nine, when the first bomb struck, the first massacre, and so, seeing that you have these essential coordinates down, which I can't keep track of because I'm confused, you could lend a hand. Is that what you want to hear? Well, I'm not going to say it… I don't want a thing from you, I don't need your help, I can take care of myself, Tristano said he had to go to Greece, it was when it was, what do I care? – and why should you? – what's important is that Rosamunda wanted him to go to Spain with her; she said, come with me. He thought Guagliona was kidding around, so he started kidding around; why not? he answered, we'll take a fancy car, a nice white Balilla, we'll drive over the Pyrenees, the drive will be refreshing, beautiful, lots of winding roads, and I'll stop at a lookout point where you can admire the most beautiful mountains, you'll even be able to see Marmolada, where your American uncle used to take you on romantic strolls and had you lean on the alpenstock he kept in his trousers, and when I'm in the mood, I'll tell you about a gifted French writer who was also a real louse. But my uncle's you, Rosamunda says, silly Clark, you haven't figured it out yet, you're here, you're telling me all this because I came to listen, you have a high fever, poor Clark, your leg's being eaten away by gangrene, you're on morphine and you didn't realize my uncle's you… sorry if under these circumstance, I thought I was your uncle… what time is it?… was I saying something?… be patient, maybe I fell asleep and I was talking in my sleep, Guagliona sometimes lays traps for me, you know? – she asks questions that catch me by surprise, she thinks my sense of my own identity has disappeared, as if I didn't know that I was the Tristano they once called Commander Clark, who became a hero… it's just that for a moment I lost consciousness and thought I was her uncle, and I was about to ask her how her American uncle is doing, I mean the handsome Cary, because I'm the one who calls him her American uncle, and you know what, I still remember how she'd answer, he's great, she'd say, he has a new wife, and he's dedicated a lyric poem to her that he sent out to relatives as a Christmas card along with a polaroid snapshot… oh, writer, I can just see them laughing like idiots in that white Balilla because Tristano said the line on the card could only be oh wife my wife, and then Guagliona continued: prepare the pot for the naughty little boy I've caught… but you mustn't think this ended in laughter, no, no, of course it's not that easy, Guagliona wanted to know more, insisted on knowing who that louse of a writer was that he'd mentioned in the Pyrenees. Tristano kept being vague about it, said he was one who'd journeyed to the belly of the night, and Guagliona, alarmed: he isn't in favor of totalitarian regimes, is he? Guagliona fixated on these things; when she parachuted in she told us the first thing you see when you arrive in New York is the Statue of Liberty… spare me the lesson, Rosamunda, it's true – we're drawn to one another, like two magnets, but that's all it is – you're the type who says one thing and does another, I'm very aware of this because in this bed where I'm rotting away, I know your past that'll be your future that I'm telling this writer, so let it be, and don't get too nitpicky, and as to the writer I said was a real louse, just be patient and listen, it's just a question of various points of view and needing to see the whole field, like this vast panorama we have before us... Be patient, my friend, I really can't remember anything more now, really, it's like everything's gone white, even so, I still want to talk, talking distracts me from my headache... I have a headache... I've gotten these things for such a long time... since the Abderites said Tristano was out of his mind... well, sure, he was so out of his mind his head exploded, just his head, but really, it was the boy who exploded... no one's ever understood headaches, the symptoms, sure, of course, and the problem of headaches, how to deal with them, how to get rid of them, but why vasodilation even exists, that's a mystery; it seems to be something neurovegetative, or psychosomatic, what they say these days; when I was younger, I wound up pounding my head against the wall... Listen, I'm going to make up the rest of the story, just to keep myself talking – see – at least I'm being honest, I'm admitting that I'm going to make things up, let's have Tristano lay his picnic out on the stone table right in the middle of the overlook, beneath two fir trees, with the horizon stretched out before them... Keep in mind, we're in the Pyrenees... the French are a clever bunch: when there's a panorama to admire they clear a space for you to park, they build a picnic shelter and bathrooms for *monsieur* and *madame*, put in two stone tables, and families can stop and eat and look out at the free, French Republican panorama, and everyone's content. Even Tristano seemed content, even without a family, he laid out a paper table-cloth and paper plates that he bought at a supermarket in Saint-Jean-de-Luz, the plates had phrases on them from famous writers or titles of famous books, and the plates he'd bought were covered with the line, *le meilleur des mondes possibles*, and at the center was a portrait sketched in deep blue of the inventor of these literary plates, a gentleman who looked like an imbecile, his cheek resting on his hand, a lock of what seemed to be tou-pee hair resting on his forehead. The brand name, in small let-ters on the rim, said, *se nourrir de littérature*. Guagliona, Tristano said, I have this feeling we might be ahead of our time. You're the one ahead, she answered, you and time don't get along too well, sometimes you go backwards, sometimes you jump around, you're not too consistent. Tristano smiled, because the view was pleasant, and also because the view seemed to be smiling, smil-ing at everyone who passed that way, it was important to notice, and Tristano noticed, and smiled back... Evening was falling over that smiling Pyrenéan valley and the light was turning slightly blue, and Tristano was enjoying the serene night air and said he loved that writer who was so infested and mean, because that writer had actually become a louse, had sucked men's blood and understood it was filthy and then he said, oh, evening was dear to him when it came, because he had a real soft spot for that poem. Guagliona nodded because apparently when evening came, it was dear to her as well, and then she wanted to know, if he called that writer a louse and thought he was so negative and hopeless, then why did he like him? And Tristano stared down at his now dirty paper plate with its quote from Voltaire, you know, he said, it's because he dove headlong into the shit of this century of ours, and diving into shit takes courage; look, when we get to Spain, I'll make you live an as-if, then if you feel like it, you can read it to yourself, but with me, you'll live it as if we're on the page, you'll see, there's a level crossing, a train that never comes, a still afternoon and a still life, and a man and a woman who sit drinking beer and watching flies, they've both had an abortion, the two of them, in their own way, and behind that crossing bar, there are hills like white elephants, a cemetery of elephants with vitiligo…

…I'd like to speak of this memory, but it's so faded now, I can still just recall the eyes: blue, I think they were… that's what the Greek poet says… he got it right… he wrote poems about the voice and lost his own… died of throat cancer… great poems… he liked men… if Tristano had met him… if their lives had coincided, if he hadn't loved women exclusively, if that's what he liked, a man like that, he could have loved him the way that poet wanted to be loved, because he was so fond of him… too many ifs: you can't do life over… but I was speaking of eyes, luckily everything becomes a tune when you reach the point where all you can do is stare at the ceiling… *j'ai la mémoire qui flanche, je me souviens plus très bien de quelle couleur étaient ses yeux, étaient-ils verts ou bleus?…* Tristano got a letter once, maybe one day I'll tell you more, there were words to a song in that letter, too, but it was a letter that was just a voice, like those the Greek poet heard… And maybe faraway faraway in time, maybe one day in someone else's eyes, you might find a little something of my eyes…

In the entranceway, Tristano could already tell he was there. He's whimpering, he said, do you hear him, Rosamunda? It was one of those real dog days of August, like they can have in Spain, and the city was deserted. Sunday, everyone gone, far away from that intense heat that settled into the stones, the asphalt, a phantom city, the museum phantom-like as well, solitary, the first paintings, like ghosts floating through a dream. Ooo, he called softly. The main hall repeated, Ooooooo, and was welcomed by the empty halls. And he remembered a white village on the coast, a wedding banquet, his mother holding his hand, the smile on the face of the parish priest and his mother saying, I hope it's all right, Don Velio, that we're not getting married in the church, Tristano wanted it this way – not that he has anything against priests – we're only just getting married now because he's been so ill, he was held prisoner in Austria and then he caught the Spanish flu, he thought he'd never come back, but he did come back a number of years after the war was over, and that's when he learned he had a son, a little boy now, but we're so grateful you've come to lunch, Signor Curate, it's so kind of you, sir… He approached a jovial-looking prelate, but he was a painted prelate, oily, fat, and merry for centuries. Tristano whispered into Guagliona's ear, Rosamunda, I never told you, my father's name was Tristano and I was never baptized. But I was, Rosamunda whispered back; up in the mountains, I know you thought I was unflappable, a real female soldier, but I wasn't, because I'm a good Christian, and I know you shouldn't desire anyone else's woman. I know you never desired women – you're a good Catholic, after all, even if you are Protestant – you've always desired another woman's man. They continued in the empty gallery; Tristano led the way like a tour guide with no one to guide, and headed up the stairs. Don't bother with the other paintings, he said, they don't concern us – not today – maybe you'll come alone some other day and look around at all the beauty here, that will be your faded springtime, but today we're going to visit the yellow dog – can't you hear him crying? – I think he's dying of thirst, let's get him some water, who knows how many people walk by him all year long, and look at him indifferently, like you do a dog, and don't give him even a drop of water, but today's the day, not a soul around, I think the guard's even asleep in his chair, if I were the director of this museum, I'd insist there always had to be a fresh bowl of water in front of that dog, but museum directors don't care what their paint-ings want, are just concerned with doing their job, they don't give a shit if this dog goes on suffering forever, like the painter wanted… The guard was sleeping, as Tristano had predicted. They went in, and the dog stared at them with the imploring eyes of a little yellow dog buried up to the neck in sand, put there to suffer so we would know for *sæcula sæculorum* how creatures with no voice suffer, and that's all of us, really, or nearly all. Guagliona looked at the dog, then she turned away, leaned against the wall, and hid her face on her arm. It's unbearable, she said, I can't look. It's just at the sand baths, Tristano said, the painter's having him take a sand bath. Please stop talking, she said. You think electroshock in the nuthouse is any better? he said, you know, it was only a little lost dog, a foundling, I'm sure, a *figlio di enne enne*, father unknown, wandering around the outskirts of the city, a bag over his shoulder, a mouthful of bread, sleeping in cardboard boxes, not even going to the dog barber, in other words, really down and *out*, and so the painter decided to do something useful for society and for his prince, he came by with the snare of his palette, caught the dog, and buried him up to the neck in sand: now you'll learn, stray dog, no more biting anyone, the streets are calm, the citizens can sleep in peace and the monarch is happy. He was cruel, Rosamunda said, a cruel painter. No, Tristano corrected her, he was kind, he was only cruel to himself, he was a loose dog. The gallery felt oppressive, smelled of mold and people's breathing from the day before. I wish there was air conditioning, she said. Oh, come on, Rosamunda, Tristano said, we're talking about Spain now: the Caudillo doesn't give a shit about modernity – or about you Americans – he's thinking about defending the West from communism, and sooner or later, just wait, someone will say this, and you think he gives a shit about air conditioning? – he'd settle for the cool of the vestry. They sat down on the floor. Tristano looked the dog in the eye, Guagliona glanced at him now and then, Tristano wasn't sure what to say, and he asked himself why he'd brought her to see that painting... You know, writer, if Tristano had the gift of prophecy, he'd have told her that one day they'd see that dog again, he'd have said, Rosamunda, one day you'll recognize that dog, and also, it's not male, it's female, it's hard to tell the sex of a dog buried in the sand, but I know it's female... Tristano didn't have the gift of prophecy, though, and that's why I'm telling you what I should have sensed, because certain signals need to be understood at the right time, and not when you're dying... You feel okay? Rosamunda asked. Like I'm dying, he answered, like I'm dying. Well, you don't seem like it, she whispered, your color's good and after lunch you were brave enough to do it three times in a row, after devouring a whole platter of Madrid tripe. Tristano ordered her to stay put, stay where you are, Guagliona, my girl, he went over to the yellow dog, he dropped to his knees, arms sagging, like a puppet with its strings cut, one day in a restaurant outside of time and space, they served me love like cold tripe, and I told the missionary cook, thank you, but I would have preferred my tripe warm, tripe wasn't a dish best served cold, I didn't eat it, I didn't want a different dish, I paid the bill and left. What are you talking about? Rosamunda said. It's something Frau reads to me, he answered, but it's not worth getting stuck on the details, it was a Pindaric flight, not important, I was talking about something to come, not last night. Then he straightened up and stood at attention in front of the dog. Commander Clark, he said, I've brought you the water you needed. He had a *calabaza* hanging from his belt, one of those empty gourds Castilian shepherds carried for fresh water, and he set it down in front of the painting, stepped back, and saluted. Let's go, Guagliona, he said, it's getting late, and the guard will want to close this cemetery.

…Let's forget time exists and not count the days we have left; if we weren't stupid enough to do that before, then let's not start now, Mavri, it feels like I was dreaming and then I awoke and asked myself where I was, was it I, was I the same, and why?… but there are no reasons why, things happen on their own, without reasons, even if in dreams begins responsibility, that old line is right, tell me about your childhood, Mavri, and your friends, those who never reawakened like I did and are now in unmarked graves up in the mountains, they belong to the people of dreams, I don't know how to talk with them… I'd like you to play that piece you played for me that night, but there's no piano here, and I'm ashamed to ask you anyway, I hear it playing in the cypresses, let's go to Cape Suonio, I want a view of the Aegean Sea from the Temple of Poseidon, your friends can't see anymore, they have empty eye sockets, they lie among the thorn bushes and nourish the roots of the chestnut trees, they called out to me a long while, but I didn't listen; Mavri, we belonged to each other though we didn't know it, these are my stones, thanks to them, I understood, stones teach us many things, maybe someday you'll come with me, but for now, let me stay, take me to Crete, I want to see the house where you were born, don't let it lie abandoned, it would almost be like your mother and father were twice dead, I'll be the one to open that door again, you'll step inside with me, I've imagined it so often, I feel I've lived there: the key's hanging from a nail on the porch behind a dry laurel branch, it's a large, heavy key to the inside wooden bolt, the first room you enter is spacious, that's where they had the oil press, there are straw-bottom chairs, but by the window is a stone bench covered in Cretan-cloth cushions, and in the middle of the room is the table where your family ate, an enormous round stone used at one time for pressing olives, set on top of another stone… this will be our workshop, we'll design our world there, put our books together on that stone… Mavri, I don't want to spend my life in university lecture halls or my nights in an observatory searching the sky, because this world isn't enough to discover other worlds, besides, look what we've done to it… I know you'll leave me often, but when you return from giving your concerts, you'll find me sitting there, on that stone… I hear a player piano, do you hear it, too?… writer, I'm talking to you… sorry, I was dreaming and a player piano woke me, but maybe I was dreaming about the player piano, too, and now it's continuing outside my dream, it's a waltz – you hear it?… Don't tell me I'm just hallucinating, indulge me, it's a waltz in A major, far away, but if you want to, you can easily hear it… it's not a player piano, though, it's a street organ, what the gypsies played at fairs when I was a boy… During the fireworks for the

88

San Giovanni Festival, a gypsy played a barrel organ in piazza San Nicolò, he'd turn the crank and people would start to dance... No one cares about these old stories anymore, but praised be the poor song from the past that brings back long-dead days... that tireless pendulum clock on the bureau always has its eyes wide open, never even closes them at night, is spying every second, like a spider spies on flies, and the universe is there, galaxies and light-years, of course, one second after another, tick-tock, and the hour's done... the gypsy heads off to another fair, always playing the same music, does another couple want to dance?... I know those two over there, she's wearing white shoes and a blue pleated skirt, he's left his jacket hanging on a chair and rolled up his shirtsleeves; ask her to dance... make her laugh, boy, can't you see how her eyes sparkle, the lights of the square flicker inside them, Chinese paper lanterns, a bouzouki player's just arrived, an old man who understands lovers, he's seen so many of them dancing in his lifetime, this old man understands everything, he's started to play "Tha Xanarthis"... of course you'll come back, the woman says, you're already back, and she laughs, she curls her hand around his neck and draws him close, people are clapping, they've made a circle around them, she runs her fingers through his hair and then she kisses him, other musicians have arrived, a lively scene now, everyone starts dancing, an old man is dancing by himself, hands raised, as though he's clutching the air, and only his feet in leather boots are dancing, these two are frozen in the crush of dancers, they're like a statue of two bodies the sculptor's extracted from one stone, they keep their eyes closed, their foreheads drawn together as though they're exchanging thoughts, thinking the same thing, that the boat for Crete departs tomorrow morning at seven and there's a festival in Piraeus, so why bother going back to the city to sleep... I know a boarding house down by the harbor, Daphne says, when my grandfather came to study in Athens he stayed there, now it's owned by Stratis, who's from my town, I'd like to go and say hello, he knew me as a girl, I think he'd be happy to see me with you, Tristano.

You never did get that big fly out of here, you're a liar just like Frau, can't you hear it – or do you think my own ears are buzzing? – maybe they are, but what I'm hearing is a big fly, I know I'm right, get it out of here, open the shutters a little, you'll see, it'll find its way out, that much light won't bother me, I'll close my eyes, what time is it, is it already past noon? It's afternoon, must be three, mmm, it feels like afternoon... strange, even from this bed, I can tell it's afternoon – I can hear it – the afternoon has its own way of breathing, its own fragrance, a sound and a sniff, and there's also a rooster that starts crowing in the afternoon, stupid rooster, what's he got to crow about? – thinks he's so brave, but he's not brave at all, just puffed up and stupid, there were two men up in those mountains once, both brave men, fighting the same battle, but they were divided about the future of their country, he was one of them, behind that boulder, staring at a flower, the three western brigades would pass to his command, but he had to become a hero first, it's not remotely easy to become a hero: a millimeter to the right and you're a hero, a millimeter to the left and you're a coward, it's a matter of millimeters, he was there, staring at a flower, and the countryside before him was his arena, would he win the fight or shit his pants?… that can happen, you're about to be a hero and everything turns to shit… Please, open the shutters, it must be evening already, I know, I was wrong before… are you getting all this down?… get it down word for word, you're free to write other things the way you want, but not this part, no, write down my every word… Open the shutters a little, let the breeze in… heroism often – no – nearly always turns to shit – but you can't say this, you can't bring children up on this, how would you put your hand over your heart, because after heroism you have to put your hand over your heart, when you stand before the flag, you stand there, waiting for that cross on your chest, the authorities all lined up in front of you… war cross… not just any fucking medal… there's the president of the Republic with his wife, Christ, what a pair, Tristano is watching them, luckily it's just an *Incom Weekly* newsreel in black and white, and the lack of color makes the scene less awful, all the other authorities are there on the stand for the occasion: the Minister of the Interior, the Defense Minister, a general weighed down by all the medals on his chest, the cardinal, maybe even two cardinals, the band with their plumes; next Sunday this solemn ceremony of homeland heroism will be shown in all the movie theaters in Italy, or at least in the big cities, before that gripping American movie where she says that after all, tomorrow is another day, with that blood-red sunset in the background... and that *Incom Weekly* newsreel is historical, because younger generations have to know that what we have here is a national hero being decorated, yes, and he was really the one who performed this act of heroism, but that isn't him, he's like the unknown soldier, he represents all Italians, even we presidents and generals who weren't in the Resistance, he represents us all, because the Italians were never fascists, and we recognize ourselves in him, the Italians always fought against fascism, always, they never dreamed of being fascists, not the Italians... I was the one dreaming, Tristano thinks, I wasn't fighting against anyone, the fascists never existed, they were all in my imagination... the crooked president comes straight toward him accompanied by a high official who carries the war cross on a silver platter, they're all banded together, Tristano; there's no escape, Tristano thinks, now I'll run away, that dawn back then I didn't run away, I stayed behind that boulder and held on to my submachine gun, but now I'll run away, it's now or never, run, Tristano, run, or in a little while you'll be a hero to these people, their equal, and it will all be over, irreversible... Writer, open the window, throw it wide open, I want to feel the cool of the evening, because the evening is dear to me when it comes, did they teach you that poem in school?, you must have had some nobody teacher who taught you that one, Tristano could have used some cool himself; instead he was sweating, the heat was unbearable, open my window, writer, let the cool night in, ah, night, it's night that should be praised, far more than evening, but it takes guts to praise the night, because the night brings dreams, and often nightmares, and it's hard to face your nightmares, harder than facing the Nazis, that's when you really see if you're a hero; now, please let me be, I want to see if I can sleep.


I knew it was her, even when she was just a figure on the horizon, a bug, because I could make out those familiar, ample hips like an amphora vase where I'd laid my hands and my body; to the left, on the hill, were two Ionic columns, of course I knew they were really the towers from my window, but the painter who'd created this scene, who paints dreams, had transformed these towers into two Ionic columns, and little by little, getting closer, her legs also seemed like two columns, and a delicate vine climbed up to cover her pubis, and he wondered if she hadn't become a tree, though the tree was moving, he was in his shroud, in the middle of this room that was flung wide open to the countryside, it was an idea of a room and inside this idea of a room was an olive grove that could only be the grove of Delphi, because the trunks were so gnarled and ancient, they could only be those of Delphi, the places they'd passed through in their life dancing dances with immemorial movements though not a trace remains, to the sound of a reed flute that we never hear, that guides our dancing, he hummed "Tha Xanarthis," and she peeked out from behind an olive tree and said, of course I'm back, I had to come back, my darling Tristano, I thought you

93

were dead, I looked all over the islands for you, I wrote you a letter, then let the wind take it, then a firefly wandering in a field of reaped wheat told me you were here, Tristano, and so I came. It's true, he said, Mavri, my love, the wheat's been threshed and the sheaves are yellowing in the fields, but it's never too late to revive the stalks. Saying this, he lifted his shroud, she was very close now and with his head bowed, he whispered, do you see? – my leg's being devoured by gangrene, the flesh is rotten and the worm is in the fruit; it's so bad, the worm is in the fruit. He was naked, with just a kerchief around his neck like the reapers wear in the field. Tristano, she said, I can still see your cock, so you're not completely rotten yet, maybe there's still a little time. Daphne, he said, how notarial our life is, I'm here in *articulo mortis*. Well, I like you all the same, she said, even if your legs are full of maggots: your trunk is healthy, and that is where your heart is beating. Then they lay down, and the countryside around them turned into a hot, wide-open plain; over the hills the orange light of the setting sun sent the shadow of the Ionic temple all the way down to Daphne's belly. You know, Daphne, he said, I forgot about backlighting, about the candle I always kept lit in a house on the shore, and one night you walked by in the frame of the window as though you were walking on air, that's the most important memory of my whole life, and I was about to forget it, do you remember that house we once lived in, the empty rooms, the piano on the ground floor, the sound of the surf, the smell of algae that I called the smell of aldae because the woman who came to clean for us was named Alda? She didn't answer, her breath came rushing in his ear, like panting, here I am, she breathed like she did at certain moments, here I am, Tristano, hold me tight, and just then the beacon light came on from down the coast, the plain was dark by then, but luckily the beacon light was on, and there was nothing to be afraid of.

...Do you know that poem where a mother dressed in black is crying over the body of her son killed in the square? Or did I already ask you? Frau read it to me the other day... you left one morning in May, it goes, and now the fountain is dry, I wish you water forever... and then it goes on to say that she unties her white hair and covers that withered flower of a face... half past midnight, the hours go by quickly, even if it isn't half past midnight, that's what I'm guessing, Frau turned on the lamp at nine, I've been here, not moving, not talking, and who would I talk to? – I'm alone in this house now... did you notice how nicely that poem works for me?... seems like it was written just for me, like the writer knew... but it's not true that I don't have anyone now, I can talk to you, even if all you do is listen, that's something, that's plenty... Thank you.

Writer, you see how I go back and forth in time, I wander, can't tell now from then, can't separate the two, which brings Papee to mind – but who was Papee? – did I ever meet him? Maybe he was a character in some novel I read once, a nice boy who fought for his country's freedom, Burundi, or somewhere like that, and the memory sweeps everything along with it, into the same water, but you have an advantage: I'm teaching you that a clock's time doesn't run at the same pace as a lifetime, and any time you'll have to discuss this, you can say you learned it from an old man about to croak who went back and forth in time as he pleased, and there will be those who think this is a trick of some kind, because they don't care if they understand, they'll think it's all a trick, and that memory… There are so few memories remaining to us, writer: Caesar's commentaries, Augustine's confessions, certain *de profundis*, like Molly's, a *de profundis* of the womb, though a man wrote it, and mine too is a *de profundis*… you know, writer, I'd really like to have a womb, to be a woman now, a beautiful, ripe young woman, the sap circulating in my body, how beautiful… lifted by the moon like the tides, a woman who was the origin of the world, and here I am instead, my two dried-up balls being devoured by gangrene, while I lie here blowing a bunch of hot air.


…Rosamunda, Rosamunda, on such a lovely evening, I truly am believing it's fairy dust I'm breathing, a thousand voices, thousand choices, thousand hearts are all rejoicing, such happiness is ours, such joy beneath the stars… Oh, wri-ter, all of my love is for you, oh, wri-ter, I'm thinking only of you… You know, it's really strange: I called you and I was only thinking about myself, I really wasn't thinking about you, and since you've been here, even though you haven't said a word, I've started thinking about you. For one reason: you're writing me. And at times, you seem to *be* me a little, and so I ask myself if what I'm telling you is mine because I'm telling it, or is it yours because you're writing it... Do things belong to those who say them or to those who write them? What do you think? Think it over – what's it matter to me – why should I give a damn at this point?


You and I need to make a pact. I thought about it all night... what I mean is, I have something to ask you, too, so thinking about it some more, I want to do a little bartering. But first let's be clear on something, because I don't want you to convince yourself that I was the one who asked you to come... it was you, you know that better than me, I whistled and you came running, because that's all you were waiting for... it was just too tempting... Sorry I'm only telling you this now, agreements should be worked out early on, like gentlemen do, sealing the deal with a handshake, but I was saying, and then I got a bit lost, even if I wanted to tell you first thing, believe me... okay, here it is... what I propose is that you say something in return... I want us to make a pact here, because I know you writers, at just the right moment, you'll see something, maybe it stands out, you think something like this has nothing to do with the rest of the story, it interrupts the flow, and so long, into the garbage it goes... I'm telling this story but you're the one writing it down, and who's to guarantee you'll include something if you think it's insignificant and doesn't matter?… But it does matter, it matters a great deal, and that's why we need to make a pact: I tell you what I promised to tell you, but you write this detail down, because they say when something's written down, it holds a different value… and be sure they know that it's not just anybody asking for this; it's a national hero, someone with a war cross on his chest, and who knows, maybe that'll impress the British, the British value heroism, they've practiced it quite lavishly, and if they hadn't been up there when Tristano was in the mountains… you can write this down: that Tristano truly admired them at that time… less at other times… because of what they did in other places, and you don't have to go very far, just think of Daphne's country, where they propped up that big fascist Field Marshall Papagos, so the Greeks got themselves a new Duce and a new king, after Metaxas, it's the British concept of democracy in other people's houses… But now let's get down to it… personally, I don't know the exact words to use – that's your job – it'll take tact and diplomacy, otherwise what kind of writer would you be… It's about the Parthenon marbles… that's what Tristano wants you to ask for, the marble friezes taken by a British lord who was ambassador to Turkey when the Ottomans controlled Greece, and who had the Parthenon flayed and the marbles transported to Great Britain, like a man who finds a lady lying unconscious on a deserted street and tears off her necklace for his wife… it was that exactly… flayed, that's the word, writer, that thief had his workers use pick axes and sledgehammers… years ago I read an account of someone who witnessed that rape, but I'll spare you the details… You know, they didn't just take a painting, what you'd stick on a wall, they stole a whole landscape… supporters of this theft have their various views… I know: the friezes at the British Museum are gorgeously lit… as if fluorescent lights in England were somehow brighter than the sun in Greece… or that when the lord took them they weren't friezes on the original temple anymore, because the Ottomans had turned it into a mosque… nice reasoning, but the Ottomans only changed the contents, a small thing – what's it take to substitute one god for another? – they didn't change the container in the least… such sweethearts, I'd really like to see how they'd react, these fine thinkers, if the spires of their Westminster Abbey wound up in the Athens Museum… The lord in question was Elgin, *Lord Elgin*, write it down, so the British won't get him confused with some other lord, with all those lords they have in England… In short, write down that Tristano wants them to give those marbles back to their rightful owner, that it's a sublime temple, and if Athena hadn't built it, they wouldn't have their House of Lords, they'd still be just a bunch of sheep herders… and maybe remind them of Byron, who died for these things, who knows, maybe that'll have an impact… And if you want, add that along with the reasonable demands of normal diplomacy, these friezes were already requested by a great poet, though no one knew him because he lived like a nobody in rented rooms, Mr. Cavafy, and that Tristano wishes to repeat this poet's polite request, which he made a century ago, so by now, it must have reached British ears… All right, here's my proposal: I tell you what you want to know, and you write down Tristano's wish, I think you're the one who's getting the better end of things... Is it a deal? If it's a deal, I trust you, it's an old-fashioned pact, between gentlemen... a verbal pact... but for us everything is verbal, everything's composed of words, right? A *gentlemen's agreement*, as the British say... If it's a deal, take my hand, I still know how to shake someone's hand, and this will be the first time you ever touched me.

Do you know what a headache means? I'm not talking about a migraine, or a slight headache, this is something else again, it's a bunch of different things at once, and it's not easy explaining something that's a bunch of different things at once... first off it's a small noise, that's how it starts, a strange bell, more like a whistle or a squeal, a sonar that arrives from far away, from deep, deep down, and you can feel it, and all of a sudden you see the fierce outlines of things, as if that whistle's there in sight, intensifying, distorting, and you feel as if a prism has replaced your eyes, because contours, edges, objects have increased and filled up space, expanded, changed shape, and through this change, they no longer mean what they used to mean, the wardrobe, for instance, is now a cube, a cube and nothing more, it no longer has the sense of a wardrobe, and now everything is rippling, space is swelling like the tide, and here comes the ache of the headache sea, like a blowing bellows that you're sitting on, swaying, you have to sit, and the floor turns fluid, and around you is a breathing lung that seems to be the entire universe, no, it's inside you, and you're on top and inside at the same time; you're a dust mote floating in the alveoli of a monstrous lung that's breathing in and out and you press on your temples, trying to hold back the waves bursting in your head like a tempest where you drown… this, this is a headache… Tristano had his first headache one August tenth, many things have happened to him, to Tristano, in August, his life is marked by August, there are men like that, it's Uranus, Saturn, so many things, I've forgotten many of them, but not this, that would be impossible, August tenth is San Lorenzo Day, the day of shooting stars, and maybe one dropped right on his head, a meteorite, but it wasn't at night, it was noon, and he was right here in this house where he'd come back to do nothing, sitting under the pergola, and he was staring at a bunch of unripe grapes, counting them off like the years of his life, one grape one grape one grape for you, he whispered, a silly little ditty, and there were already so many grapes, and right then he grew aware of a strange whistle he'd never heard before, the bunch of grapes stopped being a bunch of grapes, the air cracked into fissures, nausea rose in his throat, and he staggered across the veranda as though he were on the quarterdeck of a ship tossing in the waves, and he reached his room, closed the shutters, threw himself onto the bed and clutched his pillow, and he was off on the first of those wretched journeys that would accompany him a long while, through miasmas, locust-filled clouds, a glaring expanse of nothing in all directions… He died the day before, you know, he blew up, with his instruments of death – his boy – that he loved more than a son… goddamn him…


…Some nights, sometimes, he'd stare at the lights on the plains and think of the past, of those days when people were playing with the future of his country, up in the mountains… everyone against the Nazi-Fascists, that was clear, but the future was something else again. By now, I'm very much aware that as far as the future's concerned, there are many, could be many, like the color spectrum, slight gradations of color, almost nothing, a shade of blue will bring you to indigo, then violet, but blue's one thing and violet another, almost nothing, but try living in one shade, you'll see how intense it can be… During that time, though, he saw the world as binary; you know, we tend to be binary by nature, and we let ourselves be convinced, we're such idiots: black and white, hot and cold, male and female. In short: this or that. But why do we always have to think of life as this or that, did you ever ask yourself why, writer? I think you have, and that might be why I called you here. But back then, he saw the future as divided in two, because he thought history was divided in two – the idiot – he didn't understand that we make history, that we build it with our own two hands, it's our own invention, and we could build another, if we just wanted to, if we just convinced ourselves that history, her story, is this or that, if we only had the strength to tell her, you're nothing, madam history, don't be so arrogant, you're just my hypothesis, and if you don't mind, madam, I'm going to invent you now as I see fit. But to say this, you have to be old and useless, practically a corpse like me, before you understand that she was an illusion, a ghost, and you can't make her anymore, she's already been made. History's like love, a kind of music, and you're the musician, and while you play her, you're extremely capable, an interpreter who blows full blast on his toy trumpet or scrapes his bow ecstatically across the strings… magnificent, a perfect execution, applause. But you don't know the score. And you only understand this later, much later, after the music's already disappeared… So for him, there were only two possible futures. The first he knew all too well because he knew the country that had invented it, though you couldn't say this in Italy, a future composed of ashen days, steered by a political system that considered people not as individuals but as cogs in a superior machine, small teeth in small, insignificant wheels grinding for the great wheel, for a classless society where we'd all be equal, with equal thoughts, equal efforts, equal joys, equal destinies. You want a little happiness, what you've got coming to you, comrade? – do you have a party membership card? – a ration card for collective happiness? – very good, how many in your family? – four, let's see now… let's see now… four, you, your female comrade and two children, good, good, comrade, good, good – and your wife's card? – good, good – and your children's? – good, good – everything seems in order, comrade, you have the right to four shares of happiness:

sign here and I'll stamp your paper, you're a good comrade, and the great comrade who accompanies us all in the pursuit of happiness loves good comrades like you and wants you to have the necessary amount of happiness, just the right amount of happiness for the just world we're building, a just world for a just society built by just comrades just like you, dear comrade, that's what the great comrade said in his last speech, you must have heard it, a speech directed at good comrades like you working for a just society who deserve their just share of happiness, so what more do you want, comrade? – you've already been stamped by the political system, everything's in order, regulated, go back to your laborious home, tell your domestic comrades that the great comrade sends his fraternal salute, now, how 'bout you stop breaking my balls? – ah, yes, you fought in the mountains, you killed a squad of fascists all by yourself – you're a real hero, comrade – but if I'm not mistaken, you already got your medal for that – and you also lost two fingers – they got jammed in the submachine gun – no, don't bother showing me your hand – it's right here on this piece of paper – this piece of paper, comrade, is more important than your hand – well, you didn't lose your balls, dear comrade – sorry to be so familiar, but we're both comrades here, brave comrades like you don't lose their balls, I know, I know, there were two gladiators in the arena, one was strong, mighty, ferocious, but the other was fearless, and he had this tiny, wicked smile that made him look like an American actor, some gladiators are strong but stupid, comrade – they puff out their chest, strut around, and wind up losing their balls, because

they're stupid, but you, comrade, you're brave and you're sharp –
you're especially sharp – but don't try and be too sharp now,
comrade, because we know everything about you – we know you
went to live in a picture-postcard city – isn't that a bit aesthete? –
we know you have a good wife, but that she's not enough for
you; comrade, you say you love freedom and justice, but isn't
that a touch middle-class? – sorry to be blunt – but you seem a
bit bourgeois; you know, libertarian ideology was revolutionary
at first, but if you practice it in secret, that's just bourgeois, and
above all, we believe in the family – the family is the revolutionary center of the revolutionary society – comrade, I don't want
you to disturb the great comrade, because he's watching over
us, he only sleeps two hours a night, because he has to take care
of us all; in his feverish, sleepless nights, from his window overlooking the vast piazza where he assembled the military review
dedicated to veterans like you who saved the country, well, comrade, he's watching you from that window, and he knows what
you did on the dawn of that day that was crucial for our country,
that you took out an entire enemy squad, he knows it better than
you do, comrade, but excuse me, comrade, how many hours of
sleep do you get a night? – seven hours? – seven hours is a lot,
comrade, a whole night's sleep – he sleeps one, two hours at the
most – you don't want to disturb the great comrade – comrade,
seven hours of sleep is a good amount – we found out you write
poetry, and this makes us happy, but watch the intimism, we
know about the intimist poets, they create the past – watch
out – you don't want to drink too much past, comrade, it might

go to your head, and now, back to your busy little home where your lady comrade's waiting for you, go in peace, comrade, and don't pester us again...

...and then it goes... I saw other riddles like bloomed flowers in an empty place, empty gowns laying claim to bodies turned to air, and I saw a girl's heart forgotten in a cage, lion feces, the circus gone away, and time a fortress built of stone and stupor, and on the fortress walls a blind dove perched, but how do you decipher what heroes won't tell, how do you defeat the sea if you're free to sail but not to build a boat?... That long, annoying poem of Frau's came back to me, but you don't give a damn. I do, though: I'd like March sprinkles, but it's August instead, she says, and there's nothing you can do. And she's right...

...I'm tired but I haven't finished, let me rest a bit, but don't go – stay – keep your ears open, it's important, because there's another future beyond the one I've told you, and Tristano had to choose. And in this other future there was, simply, freedom. Which is no small thing. Here's what it looked like, up in the mountains, okay?...there were woods and a forked path and Tristano was standing in the middle of those woods, gun pointed, but he had only one gun sight, his gun fired in only one direction, it obeyed the laws of ballistics, and there's no guesswork to ballistics, because it depends on geometry, and there's not much you can do about geometry, my dear writer: if an angle's acute it's acute and if it's obtuse it's obtuse, and you don't want to fuss with angle apertures, it was truly a fork in the path, Tristano was at a crossroads, and this divided problem really came down to his rifle sight: point and pull the trigger one way, you stay in a classless society that suffocates you as a person, point and pull the trigger the other way, and the world keeps turning like always, with those who thrive and those who don't, but hey, you're on the side of freedom… it's a matter of killing one or the other, and Tristano has to choose. And you know what he chose, because you know what freedom is, you're a liberal intellectual, and you hold to your ideals, and this is why you were inspired by that interview a sneaky journalist got from Tristano, a few words, and they inspired your little book – sorry, that just slipped out – not little – short – of course it's stupid measuring novels in meters, as if quantity counts for something, truth is, your eighty pages are worth more than bricks sold by the kilogram, it's almost like you were right there at Tristano's side, up in the mountains, right there that day – even better – you're pointing the gun, you choose the direction, aim, fire. Bang. You picked democracy. Bravo. You made the same choice as Tristano, that's why you've managed to get inside his head so well – such mimetic powers – you really seem to be Tristano, in my opinion you *are* Tristano, I don't know why I'm telling you about him, you *are* Tristano, in your story, you wrote exactly what he did, you're the one who suffered what he was going through, suffered through it in first person, because you're a gifted writer, that's why I called you, in those few pages you were Tristano, a perfect Tristano, an exemplary Tristano, an indisputable Tristano that he never managed to be his entire life... How funny, in so few pages, you managed to be what a real person never was in his entire life, that's also why your novel won a prize – it should – the truth should be prized, because the truth is concrete, like that wire-haired poet said, and the truth's even more concrete when it's black on white, that, yes, that's true, you write the truth and sign it, and like Tristano, you understood the freedom you went looking for and finally found, because freedom's something to hold dear, that's for sure, and you wrote it down in black and white, and those are your words, the word is sacred, and so it must be free, but you know, my friend, there's one detail you didn't think of, and you'll need to write this detail down, because I called you to my bedside just for that, and you came to my bedside just for that, because you're curious and wanted to write Tristano's real life, and I'd like to tell you this detail... Now then, someday, if one of those creatures you sit and watch on TV in your living room, one of those creatures that's all skin and bones with a belly like a drum and eyes full of flies, if this creature steps right out of the television, materializes right in front of you, you know what you should tell him to really earn that prize you won? You don't know, do you? I'll tell you what you need to say. You need to say, speak, friend, speak – you're a free man, your word is sacred – no one can destroy your word – and this is true freedom, this is why we've always fought, all of us who love freedom, so you can speak, so you can express your free opinion – speak – my civilization will allow it, you're here to speak, you have to speak, open your mouth, brush away the flies and speak, don't give me that stupid look, do me a favor, forget that you're malnourished for the moment, forget your dumb diseases, please – speak – forget you only have one kidney for a second, it's common knowledge, organ trafficking... plus, what's one kidney compared to freedom of speech, don't waste this opportunity... your country's hit rock-bottom, it's an inferno, but a fiscal paradise for us... it's a problem, I know... you're being pillaged by our industries, your raw materials carried away... another problem the free world has to deal with... the free world backs a dictator who's slaughtered thousands of citizens – better – it's the free world who put that dictator in power, in place of the democratically elected president... a few of us, myself included, don't entirely agree on this point, and that's why I invite you to speak, speak, that's why you came into this world, to speak, the word is sacred, you're free to speak, you can trust us, I'm not just anybody: I'm a writer, and writers are very much aware of the meaning of free speech, you're free to speak with me, this person talking to you has chosen freedom, has defended freedom, stop being catatonic – speak – it's the opportunity of a lifetime, take advantage now – you might not get another chance – don't think that they're going to invite you to the broadcast transmission where the true meaning of freedom will be announced, you won't get an invitation, but here we are, face to face, in my living room, I'll consider reporting what you said, at least one word, and if you don't know how to say this word in your own language, because maybe this word doesn't exist in your own language, then say it in English so the whole world will understand; in English, the word is *freedom*, say it with me – *free-dom* – got it?... Tell him this, writer. Now do me a favor, go to bed, I want to sleep now, too, I'm tired, I'm glad Frau gave you a room with a view, those towers are beautiful, framed by the window, they're ancient, did you see how they float in the morning heat, they're almost trying to pull away from the ground, to touch the sky, they're ambitious towers, they were built in the Middle Ages, think of that – the Middle Ages – the Middle Ages means being in the middle of something, and what do you think they were in the middle of, what came before or what we are now, is there something in the middle between one thing and another? It's night out, I can tell, because I can sense the light and then the stages of the light... stages of the dark, I mean... that's what I know... Do you know the stages of the dark?


Today I've found another topic, tied to the transmission of the flesh. I'm having a philosophical moment, writer, I feel really good as a philosopher. The transmission of the flesh. You ever transmitted any? I'm sure you have, maybe into more than one uterus, that's what you modern writers do, take a wife, get her pregnant, dedicate a book to her, because a wife is a wife a wife... and then you might take another... another child, another dedication, various pollinations… .and meanwhile the printers are hard at work… the registry offices… because the human race can't be wiped out… Cain's line deserves to be transmitted… and so do the books the human race has come up with, otherwise, what's the point of this spinning globe we wander?… The transmission of the flesh provides some kind of sense to this asteroid spinning on its axis where we reside, but don't kid yourself – the world's not turning – it's just something thought up by some atheist scientist who believes in optical illusions: everything is fixed, was fixed from the start, in the sense that everything's just the same, Ptolemy was a genius, everything is fixed, how it was created or blew apart on its own, everything was born and then stayed fixed in place, we're the ones walking by, and we believe everything follows us while we walk, but everything's been fixed in place from the very start, frozen like this noonday's frozen and was frozen from the very start; do you hear the cicadas, feel the heat through the shutters, and that light inviting us to close our eyes, to abandon ourselves to the frozen ocean that pretends to move? And yet it does move… Illusions. Nothing moves, this noonday is fixed, had been, was, and will be. How many days have gone by since you came to write this voice of mine, how many days this August? No, don't bother, he won't last more than a month, the doctor said, whispered, really, to Frau in the hallway; I heard, the dying's hearing is acute, he won't last more than a month… That was early August, a Sunday, I remember it clearly because they started giving me morphine, morphine is Ptolemaic, it tends to stop everything, it crystallizes, turns time to candied fruit… Now to the point: Tristano didn't follow the obligatory path of the transmission of the flesh, he didn't want to continue in another, he spread his seed on Rosamunda's belly, and his one true love, with whom he'd wanted to share his seed, his Mavri, he abandoned on one of the Aegean islands, I'm speaking metaphorically of course, he abandoned her like Theseus abandoned Ariadne, not really knowing why, maybe because, like Theseus, he was a moron, I'm still speaking metaphorically, the myth doesn't say this – I do – Theseus was a moron. And sometimes someone does something all the same and he doesn't know why, he just does it, that's all, and then he spends the rest of his life with it gnawing away at his conscience, while he beats his head against the wall, or against a vineyard stake, the way Tristano did…

…He'd go out in the garden at night, he'd wander through the fields and the vineyard, lie down on the bare ground, pile dirt on his forehead, his own personal mourning sign, even sprinkle a little dirt in his mouth, and he'd stare up at the heavens, as he lay sprawled out, frozen, in the middle of the fields, corpse-like, though at times he'd stretch his arms toward the moon, oh moon, he cried, moon, can you hear me, sweet moon, understand me, while you wander silently across the sky, then perch, listen, moon, what wandering will be my comfort, now that my horizon's made up of endless hours and my time's not done, moon, my time's gone bad, moon, when I die there'll be nothing; my branch is dry, the seasons have passed, and the flower's died instead – why, moon, why? – moon that stirs the sap in the stalks, that makes the oceans swell, that raises creatures on the earth, parchment moon playing a fiddle, crystal moon, saffron moon, can you cast your spell, is there any place in this world where invoking you like the priests of old might renew a broken stem?, or you, powerful Persephone, who control the shores of the underworld, give back the life your crippled husband stole from me, that he's got in his smithy, he was a happy little boy who rode me piggyback under the pergola, laughing while he plucked down grapes, I loved him so, like a son, there were days in him that weren't mine, and he didn't have my skin color, his was more amber, and his hair was different, jet black, maybe from some unknown ancestors in Andalusia, but my gaze would have continued with him, a little of me still, he was all I had left of what I'd fought for, and you, moon, let this dirt put dirt in his mouth, I couldn't even give him a burial, his body was scattered who knows where, torn apart by furies, he, too, was a fury, and I didn't know, a beast, a beast, that boy who seemed so sweet, but I want him back, moon, please, I beg you, I'll teach him what I didn't know how to teach him, it's my fault, moon, I'm the one who made a mistake, I missed out, moon, and now I miss him, can I go back?... Let me relive the time I wasted – I didn't know, moon – I thought I knew it all, but I didn't know a thing...

…I was saying… before I interrupted myself… now I'm better… I was telling you something but now I can't remember, did you write it down or did you lose the thread like me? – don't lose the thread – writers mustn't lose the thread, otherwise they get off too easy, a jump in the story, an empty place… it's a mystery, people will say, the mystery of things… or there's no real conclusion, because you can't unravel the knot, and then… open-ended, and problem solved. Bravo. Get me a little water, sorry to turn you into a nurse, get the glass with the straw, otherwise I'll spill all over myself, don't call Frau, she'll interrupt us, and she'll want me to sleep, when she gives me an injection, she says I have to sleep… the fool… there'll be time enough to sleep; besides, injections have the opposite effect by now, they wake me up and I feel good, really good, I'm telling you, never better, light as a feather, no, I really am a feather… goodbye pain, goodbye guilty conscience, and who gives a shit if Tristano's so tormented by his problem, stupid Tristano, so fixated, like a fetish, but you wouldn't understand, you writers solve a problem with a snap of your fingers, a novel, a short story – olé! – like your book, how Tristano solves it in a snap, that thing over there… freedom… piece of cake, you know what he knew of freedom, you make him shift his gun sight just a few millimeters – and poof – he's found freedom… but I'm afraid the problem's not in the sight; you know, abstract is one thing, concrete's another: this thing, this freedom, is something that needs to be applied, but how? – how does someone like you – a writer – apply it? I'll tell you how… like casting out nines, or like that elementary-school rule, changing the order of the factors doesn't change the product, that's how someone like you thinks, if something's valid in one situation, it's valid for them all, because mathematics is mathematics, I read your novel about Tristano closely, I liked it, the way you apply that little rule is brilliant, you verify the rule with two different characters, the man and the woman up in the mountains, they betray each other and then are more united than ever, they had to settle in, like casting out nines, so to speak: they changed the order of the factors and the product didn't change. Ah, love, love… but no, my dear friend, there's something you never considered… changing the order of the factors does change the product. It changes day for night. Because betrayal is transitive. That's the truth. And being transitive touches others, it contaminates, circulates, expands with no logical form, no plan, no pattern… yes, there was a pattern early on, but at some point the original pattern dissolves, disintegrates, you can't consult it anymore, it was clear once, discernible, visible like everything that's visible, and then at some point it turns invisible, a shadow without limits, shapeless, like a cloud moving across the sun, forming a pool of shadow over the landscape, I'm not sure I'm explaining myself very well… Can you measure the perimeter of that shadow? You try, maybe you really labor over it, make these complicated calculations, you try to guess, and meanwhile the cloud's slipping by, so strange how the shadow has shifted a little, is now over the meadow that was filled with sunshine just a minute before, but no, it's no longer over the meadow, it's over the hillsides, go on, chase it, catch it, catch a tiger by the tail, the shadow of that cloud… That's what Tristano would think when he started thinking about that shadow, but by the time he started thinking about it, it was too late, because the shadow would already be wandering around, minding its own business, in transit, going where it wanted. And where did this shadow come from? How did it start? How was it even possible? The sun was so bright, absolutely brilliant, bringing every edge into sharp relief, no chance for error, and suddenly here's this shadow… and not only that, the weather forecast predicted continuing good weather, and Tristano himself had contributed to that report…

It's been pouring down rain… No, I'm not referring to the weather – it's scorching-hot out, just like yesterday – it's one of Frau's things, the things she reads, that says there's been driving rain all day, while this morning everything was so blue, and then it goes on, I know perfectly well how elegant a gray rain can be, and how oppressive the sun is, how vulgar, and I also know it's out of style now to be affected by changes in the light, but who said I want to be in style? These days, everyone's so sharp, don't you agree, writer?… no one's affected by changes in the light… that's just old-fashioned…

…But the topic was clouds… I was saying, how could there suddenly be a cloud going by, where did it come from, and how dare it, anyway? Someone like you wouldn't know, a writer who reads the weather by casting out nines, even if he's also produced a little humidity himself, if only through breathing, at times all you need is one little breath, the atmosphere's so sensitive, one puff and you've made your extremely modest contribution to forming a cloud, which then supplies the shadow, and suddenly the whole countryside goes dark, this morning was so radiant, really promising, but the weather's turned, who could have predicted, not a writer like you, I know your story… metaphors… your two main characters betray each other, but then they finally see the error of their ways and their betrayal cements their love even more, the music grows louder, they kiss each other passionately, the sun setting in the background, the lights go up, *the end* appears on the screen, the audience is moved, someone's crying, and now it's dinnertime, Sunday's over, everybody home. Your Tristano deserves that sort of movie, uplifting… Too bad it's not that way. Do you know what the true nature of betrayal is? – to betray, and so it also betrays the betrayer, it has no limits, like the shadow over the countryside, you begin by betraying a love, or a small love, I mean some little nothing, a cat, say, and then you wind up arriving at yourself, but you didn't know you'd get there, otherwise you wouldn't have made that first move, and it turns out it was exactly this move, this little bit of nonsense that seemed so unimportant, that's become a catastrophe, an absolute torrent, a flood that

carries you off, you're struggling, struggling, can't keep afloat…
Understand? Sure you do, you were in this country during those
times, just like Tristano, and you're not one of those people who
acted as if nothing had happened, one of those who, if he wasn't
sleeping or looking at the highest peaks of art, then laurels,
laurels, lift up your hearts… You understood as much as I did, I
mean, that someone broke his agreements, right? – and breaking
your agreement means betrayal. That's what Tristano thought,
but you didn't have him think this way in your novel, you're too
kind, and I know that's why you came running to my bedside
as soon as I called, my dear writer, because you wanted to find
out what you'd missed… you Peeping Tom… sorry to call you
that since what you really do is use your ears – be patient with
me – after all, it is pretty much the same thing; do you want to
know how Tristano started to think this way, and especially, how
he came to question why, something you didn't do, and why on
earth would you, if the principle, the ideal, was sound? So if
the principle, the ideal, was sound, that meant people had to be
killed for it? Blown sky-high? Blown to bits? Is freedom so precious, then, to be worth this price?… *Nous n'osons plus chanter
les roses*, they wrote. Do you still dare to sing them? Can you
understand how someone like Tristano thought about going to
Delphi, a ridiculous solution if there ever was one, a non-solution
solution… but what's there left to do when everything is ashes?
With no lord god of his own, he wound up putting his trust in
a senseless pilgrimage back to the origins… but the origins of
what? you might ask. I couldn't say… of his civilization that

he picked up a rifle for, or what he thought was his civilization
– *poareto di un zuanìn* – that's what we called him in dialect –
the poor little guy – the once valiant Anselmo who went off to
war with his helmet on, that helmet of freedom on his head so
he wouldn't be too badly hurt, western civilization, writer… so
let's see what you can do with this one, will it be at all like that
shadow over the countryside?… on the other side of the ocean,
another West, a torch in one hand, an atomic bomb in the other,
and insisting she's the real West – so now what? – where's the
sun going to set? All right, all right… Well… I'm tired… I'm so
tired all of a sudden, I was feeling so peppy… it must be all this
business about freedom and equality… citizen writer, I think I
heard it on our free morning broadcast, the daily reports are in
on the state of equality based on data from the national institute
for measuring freedom: the freedom stock index is down signifi-
cantly, owing to a country a little to our south that's chock-full
of poor, awful people who need a lesson on freedom, and so the
entire market has shifted south… dear listeners, we're pleased
to inform you that a branch of our stock exchange has opened
in a soccer stadium in this country's capital, with a high interest
rate; this is something our new economists developed, which
makes use of the old system, what's known as direct from the
manufacturer to the consumer: each stock index is attached
to the testicle of one of those awful customers, and every time
there's any effort to raise the local stock market, the consumer in
this country gets a nice jolt of electricity that he most unequivo-
cally feels… it's a personalized system… for those esteemed

customers of the female persuasion, the market index acts upon the ovaries, or on the fetus, in case of pregnancy… Writer, the freedom index is widespread, reaches customers the world over, our fatherland is the world over, our law is freedom, and a solemn thought is in our hearts… Go get some rest, I've kept you late. Or maybe it's not late for you, but I'm tired, anyway. Hand me the urinal first, though, set it on the nightstand where I can reach it. But don't worry, I can stick it in there on my own, I didn't call you here to humiliate you.


Ferruccio said the person who writes in order to comment on life always thinks the fact that he's commenting is more important than the comment itself, though he might not realize this. And what about you? – you write about life – so what do you think?…


…sorry for yesterday, if it was yesterday. Was it yesterday or this morning? I think it was yesterday, but I can't be sure anymore… sorry… it's true… I wasn't particularly soft on you, but you probably don't expect someone in my condition to be very nice… I know when certain things are raised… I mean, that novel's so important to you, you wrote it, even won a prize… Frau tells me you weren't feeling too well today… a headache, she says… she's taken a shine to you… you're torturing him, young sir, she tells me, hours and hours of listening to you in

this hot, airless room that stinks of disinfectant… But you don't
have a headache, I'm the one with the headache, you were just
smarting from… I needled you about your comment on life…
patience, now… anyway, sorry, I thought of a detail: when Tristano's waiting for the Germans to leave the farmhouse, you
describe his face as resembling an American actor's from back
then, and I've always asked myself how you came up with this,
how you could have known… it's impossible, that was just a
little game he had with Marilyn, no one else knew, Marilyn's the
only one who called him Clark – a coincidence? – it must be –
you're too young, and everyone who knew him in the mountains
is dead by now… I don't like that passage in your novel… Clark
waited, absolutely still, crouched for hours behind that rock;
he'd often been the prey before, but other times, like now, he'd
also played the role of the hunter… It doesn't even feel like your
writing, it's like you copied someone else, your own writing's far
more capable, it explores nuances, chiaroscuro, you're a different sort of hunter, an ambiguity detective, you're always wary,
even of yourself, you are, and here you drop me into some kind
of neorealism, as if reality's what a person sees, do you really
think life can be sealed into biography? This idea doesn't suit
you, the notion of the official record… you don't believe in biography, especially the kind that interprets and concludes, you
know these biographies are only skin-deep, you prefer lifting the
flap of skin and seeing underneath, the tissues are what interest
you, I've been mulling this over the past two days… before you
go, meaning, before I go, if you want to tell me the truth, I'd like

that… The morphine I just took hasn't done a thing for the pain, no effect whatsoever, when you leave, tell Frau she's giving me distilled water… inject him with distilled water, you'll see: it will act like a placebo… I can just hear that kid doctor who's treating my death according to local healthcare regulations… do me a favor, tell her to give me some real morphine, to put some morphine in this water clock of mine… a water clock of morphine… you like that idea? I believe in chemistry, so do you… listen to me, no, listen to someone who wrote before you, who wrote better than you, that writer who understood that even feelings are combinations of chemicals, he called them elective affinities, equilibriums predisposed by nature, understand?, it's a question of atoms, an atom of this drawn to an atom of that, valences, they combine and you either love or loathe someone, depending on… sorry, I'm losing the thread… I was saying… was it something about religion? I think I was telling you something before about religion, but maybe not, anyway, I was getting to Tristano's not believing in faith, if I can put it like that, well, he just didn't have the gift, like those with faith might say, and Tristano just didn't have it, and so he was at risk and wound up the way people like him wind up, those people who don't have anything nonexistent to believe in, and so they wind up believing in people because people exist, which is the worst thing ever, but there's also a worst of the worst of the worst, because Tristano believed in believing in people, but in my opinion, deep down, he didn't believe in them, and this is the worst of the worst of the worst – am I making any sense? And this is why at his

lowest moments, he clung oh so quietly to a faith in those reli-
gions that priests have who try to find a little happiness by rely-
ing on something like the morphine Frau's so stingy with, this
thing that lasts as long as it lasts, and as long as it lasts it's okay,
but it's not paradise, because paradise should be eternal, and
Tristano was only staying in a hotel by the hour, with just a
chance for a few good dreams. And this is why there came a
time, like I was saying before, that he decided the solution might
be to make a pilgrimage to a shrine no longer in use, a ruin that
was now a tourists-in-shorts destination, and he was thinking
that in this place the spirit of some defunct priestess might be
able to explain the past and the present and the fleeing hours,
what they might mean… life, in other words, that life you're
turning into biography, if a bit piecemeal… but I'll tell you about
this trip later, I'll remember it better tomorrow… and I'll make
it to tomorrow, don't worry, and even to the day after that, I'll let
you know when the movie's over, I'll know better than you, and
in the meantime, you stick to writing Tristano's biography, what
you can write, what's possible to write… Life… a novel read one
time only, long ago… a philosopher said that, I can't remember
who, must be German, only a German could say something so
grim and so true… speaking of lives and novels, I think I may
have left out a third type of biography, the kind that's fictional-
ized, sorry to keep on about this, but the book you wrote with
your character inspired by Tristano – when someone writes in
first person and is writing someone else's life as if it's his own –
deep down, this becomes something of that third type. Why did

you write me in first person? That might seem normal to you, but, listen, it really isn't. Why did you become Tristano? Why did you put yourself in his place? – and thirty years after it all happened, when Tristano wasn't Tristano anymore, when there was no longer a reason for it, except your personal reasons, if we can speak of these… I don't think there's a writer out there who can say why he writes – and what does your life have to do with Tristano's, anyway – why did you identify with him exactly?… Why do you write, writer? Are you afraid of dying? Do you want to be someone else? Is it a longing for the womb? Do you need a father – like you're still a child? Life's not enough for you? And where did you get the idea to write about Tristano – up in the mountains? But you were never in those mountains, not with a submachine gun in your hands, anyway, maybe you were up there on vacation, in some nice hotel with old-world, Central European charm, because the Cecco Beppe – the Franz Joseph – railway used to lead up there, I know about hotels like that and the people who go there, entrepreneurs, politicians, the rich and powerful… maybe you were surrounded by that sort and got the idea to write about Tristano – was it because you saw the Alan Ladd film *Shane*? Was this why, during that time of war, you had your Tristano obsessing over the Soviet tribunals and the Moscow Trials, why you had him act as supreme judge, in the name of a sacrosanct principle, as a condemnation of any attempt to stifle individual consciousness, a sacred principle that anyone wanting to create a free society had to recognize? But how could you simplify Tristano that way? Who are you, writer, to possess the pangs of conscience of someone you've never met? Tristano seems like one of Charlemagne's paladins, Charlemagne, the great avenger of betrayal, relentless toward traitors. But what do you know about real betrayal?... I think you just know the edges of it, the piddling stuff, nothing, what you solve with a pardon me, a bedtime confession, a transgression. You can't possibly know the very heart of betrayal... Call for Frau, call her in here, tell her that even she's betraying me, betraying me for my own good or what she thinks is my own good, such a stupid betrayal... instead of morphine she's pumping me full of distilled water, now's the time for another injection, I can tell by the light that it must be five in the evening, six at the latest, just listen to the cicadas, this is when they sing like crazy, *a las cinco de la tarde*, they're afraid the male won't come back again, they've been calling him all day... he's coming, he's coming... the male cicada always comes back, even if it's at the last moment, males keep others waiting, they're cruel, but then he returns and he finally impregnates the female, and then for her it's all over, she's served her purpose, what she sang for, the fool, he's filled her belly, she lays her eggs and croaks so another cicada will be born that will spend another summer singing, calling for the male to impregnate her... Call for Frau, let's continue this later, the pain's getting worse, and it's making me crabby... can't you see I'm in a bad mood?... and you, too, go lie down, rest at noon, pale and thoughtful, you deserve a little nap, writer, or go out to the vineyard for a breath of fresh air, since Frau says I'm keeping you prisoner in this dark room that stinks of disinfectant.

Frau read me her Sunday poem, an ancient Persian poet, she says. In my opinion it isn't Sunday, this August has too many Sundays, Frau's tacking on some more Sundays, maybe that's her way of prolonging my life, adding on Sundays... Young sir, she says, the poem starts like this: Don't think about the rotation of the Earth, Saki, first think about my head... Saki's the manservant of the old Persian poet who brings him cups of wine, part servant, part philosopher, just like Frau... Oh Saki, where did the old days go?... Tristano would have his own way of continuing the poem, something like... I'm stretched out on my deathbed, Saki, they've stuck a catheter in me that I pull out just to be spiteful, as for me, besides my voice, there's nothing left, or almost nothing left, a profile on the pillow, sharp as a razor, and some breathing that at times turns to a rattle, your master's lying out there, dear Saki, outside the window it seems like an August so still, broken only by the frenzied cicadas, how long until tomorrow, Saki, is it still a long way off?... why is it always today?... an entire month of today, make tomorrow come and carry me away, there's a big fly that keeps hitting the mirror, trying to get out, stupid fly, it can't find the way out, like me, it needs morphine, like me, I lie here and talk and talk, but why insist on digging up old days, Saki... please, don't let that young nurse in, the one Frau hired, she's here with my urinal so I won't piss the sheets, I can't bear how she slips it so delicately into that glass container, like a dying flower... Saki, it was a beautiful May day, the zephyr had returned, and Tristano was sitting on his motorcycle near a newsstand, and it felt like Italy was cured, and the whole world alongside Italy, and he was humming our fatherland is the world over, our law is freedom, and even for him, life was returning... the sap was rising, after all that wartime adrenaline, all the carnage and blood, and now, sitting on his motorcycle, he was saying, how beautiful. It was May of forty-five, I remember it like it was happening this very moment.

You know when everything really became clear to him? When everything seemed already clear and already over, on the sixth of August of forty-five. At a quarter past eight that morning, if you want to know the time as well. That day Tristano understood that after the monster was conquered came the monstrosity of the conquerors... it was the second crime against humanity in this happy century now coming to a close... that morning, the first atomic bomb used as a weapon of mass destruction was dropped on one of our cities, and that city was annihilated, two hundred thousand people incinerated. I say two hundred thousand, but that leaves out the thousands who died later, and all the stillbirths, all the cancer... and they weren't soldiers, they were defenseless citizens whose one offense was being blameless... There's a place, in Hiroshima, called Genbaku

Dome, it's a pavilion, meaning it's an atomic dome, and this was the epicenter of the explosion, and here the soil temperature reached the temperature of the surface of the sun; near the monument with its peace torch is a stone slab, a doorstep, an ordinary doorstep like you'd find in front of any of our houses, where we lay the doormat to wipe our feet. Inside that stone, that piece of marble, I imagine it's like paper absorbing ink, and there's the imprint of a body, the arms outspread. This is all that remains of the body of the man who melted on his doorstep at a quarter past eight on that sixth of August of forty-five… If you can, take a trip there, it's informative… it's been said that those victims were pointless, the monster's head had already been crushed at Dresden and Berlin, and to break Japan all the Americans needed were conventional weapons. That's a mistake, that the victims were pointless – for the conquerors, they were extremely useful – in this manner, the world would come to know its new masters… History is an icy creature, she doesn't have the slightest pity for anything or anyone; that German philosopher who committed suicide in a small hotel on the border, so escaping Franco and Hitler and everyone – maybe even escaping himself – he'd reflected too much on this ruthless lady that men court in vain, and it didn't seem to do him much good… in his reflections he wrote that when faced with an enemy, if that enemy wins, even the dead aren't safe… and I'd add that this includes all enemies, even someone who's the enemy of evil men, because being the enemy of evil men can't make someone do good – and what do you think of that?… I understand your objections, I've been too succinct, of course if evil won there'd be no way out… but speaking of good, I wanted to say… well… good, okay, good conquered evil, only there's a little too much evil in this good and a little too much imperfection in this truth… The truth's imperfect… That journalist who snuck an interview with me years ago – by pretending we were just talking over a drink – he wrote this concerning the subject: that Tristano admitted to the existence of God, but it was a short-lived existence. Too bad you didn't explore this more in your novel, it's a topic that warranted some reflection; you know, this understanding of Tristano was a bit too simple, as if what he meant was that even gods die, but we all know that: take Jupiter, for instance, who lasted a good long while before being replaced, but that's not what Tristano meant. Sure, of course, everything grows old, probably God, too, what we believe in, but God won't die a natural death, then be replaced by something else. I'm afraid he's got a more painful end coming to him, if things keep going the way they are, think about it… one day… imagine a heat like the surface of the sun, but not in just one spot, over the entire planet, thousands of Hiroshimas, a whole slew of Hiroshimas, Hiroshimas all over… an immense roar, and then an immense silence, a big bang in reverse, not a living soul left, not even a cat, everyone kaput… Sure, he'll still exist, but who cares, if no one's around anymore to believe that he exists… an unemployed God… we'll make him useless, pointless, because what's the point of having God if no one's around to believe in him?… I've gotten off track again, as usual, today I meant to tell you about our Hypnos Pages, I think without our ever saying it, we started doing this in answer to that philosopher who questioned the possibility of writing poetry after the unspeakable had occurred. Not only was it possible, it was probably the only thing we could do that made any sense, because when the monster's been conquered and you don't believe in the monster's conquerors anymore, all you're left with is believing in your own dreams… in dreams begins responsibility, like I told you, is the line we used as an epigraph in our little books, because the arm reaches only as far as the hand, but a dream can go on and on… a prosthesis slipping past the prison of existence. Seems to me we started in fifty-two, we did a book a year, so we made thirty-six, they stopped eleven years back, when the others died… Any poets that weren't Greek we all translated, Daphne and I, and her friends, Ioanna and Antheos, who signed his name as Marios because that's what I called him. Handmade, you know, with a hand press from an old print shop, a contraption once used for printing leaflets against the Ottoman Empire, that's what the man from Cyprus said who sold it to us, and it's certainly possible, the thing was gigantic, weighed a ton… Why Crete and not here at home? Your question makes sense, with a nation like ours that's full of saints, sailors, and poets… not that Crete was Paris, but people from Crete had character, you know what they did when the Germans invaded? – they wiped out an entire Nazi battalion that was armed like the Nazis always were, and you know how they did it? With their billhooks for harvesting olives – they even strangled Nazis with their bare hands… And Italy back then… you're too young, you were just a boy… Pella, Tambroni, these names won't mean much, if anything, to you, Don Gnocchi's crippled children, the Polesine flood, the processions of the penitents, the weeping madonnas… Do they still weep? Around here madonnas' tears come easy, and saints and sailors seem to be on the rise. Luckily, we've still got poets, too, but they must feel a bit uncomfortable in this company… You're a good writer, too bad you write prose… sorry, I'm not being fair, as far as I'm concerned I should be grateful you write prose, if you'd been a poet, you wouldn't be here patiently gathering all these bits and pieces I'm telling you, maybe you'd have disposed of me with an elegant elegy or a poison epigram, the kind they kill you with even after you're gone… or some little nonsense rhyme, a limerick, maybe, like the British are so good at, let's see… let me think… There was an old hero they say, Who tucked all of his dreams away, But they started to rot with the gangrene he got, So it's dreamless and legless he'll stay.


What's the time, one already, like you Northerners say? I told you to come at thirteen hundred hours but not to wake me, I was having such a good sleep and then you woke me, you're nice, but you follow orders to the letter, if you see I'm sleeping, please don't wake me, I slept two hours, one hundred and twenty minutes, I could have slept two hundred minutes, think about it, two hundred minutes less…

It was August, like I told you, a lot of things in Tristano's life happened in August, a hazy, sultry day, haze over the hills and haze on the mountain and haze over the plains, too; and even inside them, a great haze like cotton that blankets everything, is deadening. Tristano waits for her to speak, if she's come all the way here, she wants something, he stares at this woman he loved so passionately, her eyes sunken now in their sockets, darkly ringed, almost purple, like a mask, her headscarf doesn't completely hide the hair growing back at her temples, she's ten years younger than he is but looks twenty years older; still, he thinks, it feels like just yesterday that they were up in the mountains, and he showed her the yellow dog buried in sand just yesterday, and their trip to Spain, and he asks himself again, why, why Spain? Because of my work in Spain, she'd say, my friends in Spain... There's a darkness in her eyes, like fear, Tristano understands this, he knows them well, those eyes; in spite of everything, she's assumed a relaxed position on the couch, legs crossed. They're both quiet. A boy's voice is coming from the back of the house, he's speaking to Frau, who knows if Frau wanted a child. All you did was spill your sperm on my belly, I wanted your child, but you spilled your sperm on my belly, you always did that... Marilyn talks this way, they're her expressions, she's always talked like this, Tristano recalls, she didn't value the weight of her words in Italian, sometimes she talked like a sailor, other times, like a Protestant pastor. He's almost twelve, Marilyn is saying, he looks like you, did you see how much he looks like you? Not really, Tristano says, but if you say so… I picked him because he looked like you, Marilyn breathes, you're like two drops of water you're so alike, there were a lot of children, but I saw him right away… A long silence now, hard to break. Marilyn lights a cigarillo, coughs, sorry if I start to cry, she says. But she's not about to cry, maybe she's only thinking aloud. From down the hall comes a tune in German. Frau rarely sings, only on special occasions. Rosamunda, Tristano says, please try to be clear, what are you trying to say?… you picked him, there were a lot of children… Marilyn fidgets with the cigarillo between her lips, then she puts it out in her tea cup. Well, she says, there were so many wretches in wretched Spain, the orphanages were full… some still are… I adopted him, I felt so bad for him… it's true, he doesn't look like you at all, but that's not important, it's like he was your son, I always thought of him as the son you refused to give me, and now I'm entrusting him to you, please take him, I can't raise him. Maybe she's waiting for Tristano to ask her why, but he stays quiet. Then she says, I don't have much more time. She shifts her headscarf slightly for him to see. I tried what I could, she says, but the results were negative, the doctor was clear, there's nothing left to try. She's clawing her own palm but doesn't realize. On his birth certificate he's Ignacio, she adds, but I call him Clark, he's always been Clark to me. She pulls an elegant suede wallet from her purse. Here are his documents, she says and sets them on the table. Marilyn, Tristano says, I only come back periodically, I think you know that, normally just in the summer, just to keep up the vineyard and olive trees a little, Agostino can't do it all on his own, and then there's Frau, this is her house, too, by now, she's got nowhere else to go; the rest of the year, I live in Kritsa. Is that near Athens? Marilyn asks. It's a village on Crete, Tristano says. Did you see how he hugged you, she says, he loves you, I've always talked about you, he knows all about us, I told him you were his real father. You're crazy, Tristano says. You're crazy, Rosamunda, there's something wrong with you – always has been. He's speaking softly, almost to himself. Marilyn doesn't answer, she's rummaging in her purse, keeps looking, then empties it onto the couch, and finally retrieves an old square photo not much larger than a postage stamp, a young man with a wisp of hair on his forehead, wearing a military jacket, a submachine gun over his shoulder, there's a mountain farmhouse in the background, a dark patch of woods. She holds it out to Tristano. He was conceived the day I took this picture of you, she murmurs. That photo's almost twenty years old, he says, you're not well, Rosamunda, please, stop talking, you don't need to say anything more. Where I come from, Marilyn says, ignoring him, there's an old Navajo belief that when you keep thinking about a man, sooner or later, his spirit will give you a child. Frau is at the door: Ignacio wants to see the bay horse, we're going to the stable, we'll be back shortly, if the signora would like more tea I'll bring in the kettle. Marilyn's putting her things back in her purse. You could be with him in the summer, she says quickly, three months a year isn't so little, you'd be a good father to him, and you don't have children, maybe you're sterile, I'm giving you the chance to have a son who's almost yours, is practically yours – no, *is* yours – please, Tristano, raise him, I have no one left in America, my family's all dead. And what about the rest of the year? Tristano says, excuse me, Rosamunda, but who's going to look after him here in this house? She gets to her feet, staggers, knocks against the end table, tea splashes from her still-full cup. This Frau, she says… Agostino… I don't know them, but they must be good people, and during the winter he'll have school – you could find a good boarding school. Where are you going? Tristano asks. Back to Spain, she says, but the best train for Irun leaves tomorrow morning – the station's far, and I don't want to drive at night – I'll find some little hotel on the coast. She tightens her scarf under her chin, hesitates, then puts her finger to her lips, sending a kiss or telling him to be quiet, he can't be sure. Is your uncle waiting for you? he asks. We're thick as thieves now, she says, sometimes life's like that, even if you don't want it to be, I never understood why you called him my uncle – he's your age. Because he's the American uncle, Tristano answers – the classic Uncle Sam, with stars and stripes on his top hat and his pointing finger, commanding *I want you* – has he got something to do with Ignacio? I'm Ignacio's mother, Marilyn says, he wasn't involved in the adoption, but Ignacio loves him and really considers him his uncle… If Ignacio wants to visit him, you shouldn't stop him, but keep an eye on him: his uncle's in a dangerous business – so was I. She heads for the door, and Tristano follows. I'll go with you, Rosamunda, it's a long way, and

I don't want you driving through all those hills by yourself… and so it goes… Tristano didn't know that on this day, on this short trip with Marilyn, they'd find a dying dog that they'd name Vanda like the yellow dog they saw years before in a museum. But this you already know, writer, because I told you the day it popped into my head, I can't remember when that was… How strange, you're ahead of Tristano's life, let's stop here now, for today.

…Hello? Who is this?… He blew up… What are you saying?… I'm saying your boy blew up, don't you understand Italian… Who are you?… Never mind, I'm someone who knew him better than you did, but enough with the questions, listen and be quiet, listen now, he had the thing in his bag, and it blew up between his legs, the idiot, not too sharp your boy, he was all talk, plenty of philosophizing, the sun setting on the West, the decline of our civilization, but with some small jobs you need a brain, you need real smarts, one time maybe he did it all right, but that was just a matter of leaving it and getting the hell out of there, not handling anything, and that spot was easy, you just dropped the bag and left… listen, you bastard, you shot at us years ago, but we forgive you, we like you all the same, respect you, in our way, at least you didn't go on some transcendent quest to India… you listening?… you're tough, we know that, and you loved your boy, we loved him, too, we assigned him the role of Saint George slaying the dragon, the idiot democrat with communist leanings… listen, do something for me, he must have left a bunch of evidence lying around, a tad disorganized, your boy, all talk, and we put too much trust in him… you listening?… listen up, do me a favor, go to his room and have a good look around, there must be datebooks, notepads, take it all and burn it, and especially if you find anything referring to this bad ass we all called *omaccio*, with the initials om, *o* as in Otranto and *m* as in Milan – got it? – take it all and burn it – you don't want your good little boy to be exposed, right? – not with that bag that blew him up, balls first… listen now, do what I tell you… click… Youuu youuu youuu… end of call, got it, writer? End of call, for Tristano… Keep that lamp lit on the dresser, the one with the shade with the glass droplets, and lay a handkerchief over the top, I don't want to be here in the dark tonight, yes, I'll say it's night, though it might be morning, but that's your problem, for me it's night. Good night.


…and I saw my entire life reduced to that insect, a minuscule, complicated instrument for flight and hibernation, the buzzing rage and fragile beating of wing casings and filthy feet, I tossed it all into the gutter, bits of rubber, smell of burning cork, that's all that ties me to this world… You know what I'm referring to, it's that piece Frau tortured me with, it didn't just come to me, it's because Tristano started getting letters, one after another, a steady stream. But I don't feel like talking about that now, I don't feel like saying anything – but stay here anyway – please – stay here anyway and I'll have other things to tell you… you have to be patient. Be patient.


…Could you explain a bit more, said Doctor Ziegler, about what you mean when you say you feel as if everything has stopped? Tristano was sprawled in the wicker chair, one arm dangling, the other covering his eyes from the noonday sun: it's like this afternoon, he said, everything has stopped, don't you feel it?… a stillness has settled over everything, wiped out space and time, like with some medieval paintings when you see a saint in rapture, under his own mystical spell, an eternal moment… any sound at all now and the glass bell covering the countryside will crack; a rooster might crow, a dog might bark, and the spell will be broken… okay, what I mean is I have these moments when I feel like it feels this afternoon… everything has stopped… and I feel like I'm stopped in the middle of time that's stopped, as if I've been momentarily transported to another world. Even Doctor Ziegler had stopped pacing back and forth on the porch, he'd stopped beside Tristano, hands behind his back, deep in thought. Go on, Herr Tristano, go on… Or maybe I'm feeling other things, Tristano continued, like I'm dreaming though I'm awake, and forgotten memories from long ago start coming back… memories I didn't even know about… they well up so fast and flash before me like a movie projected on a wall, and it's my eyes doing the projecting. And what do you feel? Doctor Ziegler whispered, can you tell me? Tristano was quiet. Ziegler waited patiently. If you feel like sighing, the doctor whispered, then sigh... don't breathe in, sigh, sighing is what our bodies invented for expelling that diffuse, insidious anxiety from the pneuma that the British call *spleen*... yawning serves the same function, though less extreme, for common boredom, but yours is a different kind of boredom... it's a weariness of being... so sigh, Herr Tristano. Tristano breathed deeply, and he let out a long, weak sigh, as though releasing evil humors composed of air. Go on, Doctor Ziegler said. What I was referring to, Tristano said, was a very intense sense of nostalgia... too intense... devastating... but it's not nostalgia exactly, more of a yearning, something frightening, more abstract, because nostalgia implies the object you have nostalgia for, and the truth is I don't feel nostalgia for the images flashing before my eyes like a film; often, they're memories that don't matter, banalities buried in my memory because they're banal, and so they carry no nostalgia... no, the nostalgia I'm feeling is outside, unrelated to those images, I'm not sure I can explain: it feels like they're not the cause of this nostalgia but that this nostalgia is a condition, and without it I couldn't see them... so this isn't really nostalgia, it's a vague restlessness that's also become a fear of sorts, but mixed with the absurd, and inside this sense of the absurd there's a terror that's destroying me, as though my body's convulsing and about to blow apart, you must have seen in the movies how they'll bring down old city-buildings so another can go up, they collapse in on themselves, crumple, implode... that's how I feel... my body's imploding, and I feel terribly cold, my hands and feet are freezing and that's when I get a splitting migraine: ferocious, unbearable. Doctor Ziegler was sitting on the low wall by the pots of lavender, he'd plucked a flowering sprig and was brushing it over his face, breathing in the smell now and then. *Angor mortis*, the doctor murmured, that's what they called it in the ancient world... you've described the most complicated symptoms of the migraine aura, Herr Tristano, cluster headaches, probably, and they never just come on their own, when these empresses come calling, they're preceded by an ambassadorship of the most distinctive creatures, a madhouse of heralds, trumpeters, courtiers, female dancers, shouting street vendors, fire eaters, tightrope walkers... if I were to take a census of all the different kinds of auras preceding headaches, I'd be here until evening, and I'd have to insist, Herr Tristano, that you invite me to stay for dinner... I think tonight we're having rabbit with rosemary, Tristano answered, it's a dish that Agostino's wife prepares that's just sublime, and maybe Frau will make a chocolate cake. Doctor Ziegler removed the white coat he always wore, even when he saw his patient at home, and he hung it on a hook on the pergola. Chocolate's not recommended for headaches, he said, but I love it and you can avoid it, rabbit on the other hand will be fine for us both, since it's white meat.

You came here to gather up a life. But you know what you're gathering? Words. No – more like air, my friend – words are sounds composed of air. Air. You're gathering air.


The rabbit with rosemary was really quite good, Doctor Ziegler said, but this chocolate cake… we have cakes like this where I come from, but this one is something else again, maybe it's the ground almonds… you can certainly have a little, Herr Tristano, nothing's going to happen if you do. Tristano could tell what Doctor Ziegler really wanted to ask, and so he brought it up, to avoid any awkwardness: I did invite Frau to eat with us, he said, but she refused, said she was tired… the truth is, she isn't tired, but I don't want you to think she's avoiding you, either, Doctor – quite the contrary – she respects you a great deal: the truth is, I've put myself in your hands because she advised it, I mean it… the real reason is she's afraid we'll start speaking in German, which would only be natural, it's your language after all, and I don't mind speaking it, either… you see, Doctor, Frau… I understand her, she came here when she was just a little girl, and it's not that she's lost her German, but she's had to use Italian her whole life… I don't know what it is that keeps her from speaking German with a German, it's as if she has to get over some kind of hurdle, as if she's ashamed… she only speaks German with me, but imagine this, if someone annoying drops by, someone unexpected, then Frau will speak to him in German, and you should hear how good her German is then, and she'll pretend she doesn't know any Italian. Herr Tristano, Doctor Ziegler said, I'll allow one more bite of cake, I'm sure you'll sleep better tonight, you'll have no unwelcome visitors… but I promised you a list of the symptoms leading up to the arrival of the empress, as I call her, it's an endless list, so I'll try to be succinct… but first, this strange term, aura… it comes from an ancient physician, Pelope, who was Galen's teacher… he was the first to note the physical phenomenon generally signaling the onset of the seizure, a sensation that starts in the hand or foot and seems to rise toward the head. One of his patients described it as feeling like cold vapor, and since the general belief during that period was that blood vessels contained air, he thought the problem had to be vapor in the limbs that was then carried back in the veins and he called it *pneumatickè* aura, an immaterial vapor… Herr Tristano, when you say a star fell on your head one August night, you were really telling me the truth with that metaphor of yours… that star didn't just fall on your head, it entered inside your head, I'm sure of it… you started seeing brilliant intermittent lights with your eyes closed, zigzagging electricity, flashing lights that no doubt looked like continuously transforming mosaics, like a kaleidoscope, am I right? Tristano, silent, gave an imperceptible nod. It's the most common aura, Ziegler continued, light effects like fireworks going off inside your eyes, and even things, objects, seem to have glowing outlines, or they're bright, anyway, am I right?, as though they're encircled by an electric wire and you can see the electricity running through them… but the aura symptoms, before the empress arrives and while she's visiting, are endless... sensory hallucinations of various kinds, emotional disturbance with extreme yet indefinable emotions, impossible to describe, to communicate to others... something like ecstasy, that some even find pleasurable... who knows, perhaps many mystics suffer from terrible headaches... plus visual disorders, perceiving objects and figures as distorted, or the magnifying of an image, from what I can tell... the person in front of you looks like he's shrinking, or growing, growing all of a sudden, in front of you, like you see in certain documentaries on plant growth, you must have seen them, a camera lens is trained on a flower bud for a week, and you watch the flower blooming in a few seconds because the image has been sped up... Lewis Carroll suffered from terrible migraines and described these optical distortions extremely well with his Alice... for that matter, he was also a mathematician, and he understood logic, he knew how to talk about his symptoms logically, even if we find his logic fantastic... and then there are hallucinations of sound... noises, hissing, buzzing, muttering that can be dim or crystal-clear, it all depends, it might be the rumbling of thunder or the roar of a fountain... but it might also be voices, many voices... the most common case histories include familiar voices, those voices that are or were a part of our life, or that we've listened to so much they're stored up in our warehouse of memories... but they can also be completely unknown voices, artificial voices that our brain invents, generates. Doctor Ziegler paused. These cases are rare, complicated, Herr Tristano, I don't want you to worry, usually they occur in migraines associated with epilepsy, but they can also occur in non-epileptic subjects, very acute forms that cause convulsive seizures… however, there is some scientific debate on the matter, and in fact, some maintain that it's not convulsions that bring on the headache but the other way around… by now, Tristano was on his third piece of cake. I don't think chocolate has much to do with it, either, he said… but the symptoms I described this afternoon, memories that just come rushing out of nowhere, experiences that rush by like a movie, what can you tell me about these, Doctor Ziegler? They might belong to the category of déjà vu, the doctor answered, I'm inclined to think they belong to the category of déjà vu, in a more complex clinical context, of course, but I'd say they belong to that family of temporal confusion… there have been theories advanced concerning both the physiological and the psychological bases of this phenomenon that we've all experienced, if only momentarily, the feeling that we're reliving something for the second time… there seems to be a delay between our perception of something and the transmission of that perception to the brain – it's a millionth of a second delay, of course – but our brain thinks that years have passed, the brain's already lived through this thing – am I making myself clear? But why this should occur is still a mystery… An important physiologist defined déjà vu as a distortion of the cataloguing of time in the nervous system… such a beautiful definition. Freud, on the other hand, explored déjà vu in his studies of *Unheimlich*, what's referred to as the uncanny, because the experience of the uncanny does indeed often accompany déjà vu, though it's hard to say if it follows or precedes the incident… to Freud, déjà vu is the return of the repressed experience, which feels unwarranted, like a betrayal, and so provokes this sensation… And what theory do you support? Tristano asked. Doctor Ziegler helped himself to more cake, but to be polite, left the last bite for Tristano. Cool country air spilled in through the wide-open windows. Doctor Ziegler was preparing to leave. Since I first met you, he said, and you started this type of hybrid analysis with me, I've grown ever more convinced that the two theories aren't mutually exclusive – actually in patients like you they can be the perfect marriage… good night, Herr Tristano, try to get some rest.


I must have had a dream, I dreamt about Tristano… or maybe it was the memory of a dream… or maybe the dream of a memory… or maybe both… Ah, writer, such a rebus… Do you ever keep a recording device with you? Sorry to bring this up, but I've begun to suspect you might have a little recorder in your pocket. But did I already ask you that? Maybe I already asked you that. Well, if you have one, turn it off, I don't want my voice to linger; besides, you shouldn't record a dream, you have to listen and then rewrite it, just listen, listen close and then rewrite it, that's the start of literature, telling someone else's dream, I'm sure it'll come to you, you'll work it out in your imagination, and I'm also leaving you the point of view… we'll do it this way, the point of view is mine – well, Tristano's – because he's the one who lived it, but I dreamt it from my point of view and now I'm telling you, and then you'll tell it, and so… you, I'm sure, know these tricks better than me, but I once read a book on the topic, a manual, I've always liked manuals; you'd be surprised: for someone you consider a man of action, I've read an awful lot of manuals in my life… how to perfect your dance technique, how to learn the art of chess, how to paint with watercolors, how to use the stars to guide you, how to scale the Alps… how to screw up your entire life and not even know it… If you really think about it, the point of view belongs to the dream, in the sense that it's the dream's point of view, not mine, not Tristano's, because you can't control dreams, just like you can't control the heart, you have to live dreams the way they want to be lived, and this dream wanted me to dream Tristano, like so: Tristano was flattened out in the shrubs, I don't like that word, flattened, but if I'm not mistaken that's what you use in your novel, and Tristano is surrounded by thick brush that stretches all the way to the woods and the mountainside. And his finger's quivering on the trigger of the submachine gun, and through the sight, he fixes his right eye on the farmhouse door, because he knows the Germans will have to leave by that door, as will the traitor who brought them there. Boom, boom, boom goes Tristano's heart, and this pounding seems to carry all the way to the versants of the valley… sorry for that word, versants, it's an Alpine word, ugly, don't you think?, I hope you've never used that word… and it feels like the beating of his heart echoes off these versants, magnified, boom, boom, boom… and in the strange logic of dreams, though it's so real, Tristano sees the traitor his bullet's waiting for, the traitor is at the door, smiling and nodding for him to come inside. And Tristano obeys the relentless logic of dreams, gets to his feet and approaches... and only as he's crossing the clearing does he realize that this traitor isn't the school janitor, this traitor has the face of a woman, and he knows this woman, even if she is wearing a German uniform and has a wisp of hair on her forehead, imitating some cocky-looking guy... It's Marilyn, it's Marilyn... Tristano wants to scream, he pulls out his knife, holds it up, waves it as though to stab that cross-dressing traitor, then he slows down, like slow-motion in a movie, because in that moment the film of Tristano's dream is slipping into slow-motion, and his hand moves slowly, ever so slowly, one centimeter at a time, gently, a graceful arc, almost tender, almost a graceful dance, the blade in that hand that will tear into the traitor's lungs and bring on the death the traitor deserves, but with the logic of dreams, Tristano's hand falls to the traitor's shoulders, about to stab, and then the hand drops the knife and is resting on Rosamunda's bare shoulders, drawing her into an embrace, because that's how dreams go, writer, they take you where they please, and now he's dancing with her, that rugged mountain clearing has become a drawing room flooded with music, an Italian garden viewed from the windows, he's dancing, holding Rosamunda who's dressed like a German soldier, her breasts pressed to his chest, her nipples like stone... her arms are draped about his neck, and she's caressing him, Clark, she whispers, her tongue flits into his ear,

Clark, my darling, you're the only one I ever loved, the others were just my being wicked, just my need for some male company, some reassurance when you were on your missions, down in the valley... Tristano has his arms around her waist, and he's stroking her, and then she takes his hand, guides it toward her stomach, lower, to her groin, and now Tristano feels something hard beneath those soldier's trousers, a male organ, an erect male organ, and she wants him to stroke it, she's whispering in his ear, her voice hot, sensual, Tristano, the commander's sent me, he's not dead at all, that was all a joke, come play with us, darling, he can't do it anymore, but he still loves me, and for him to do it he needs to watch someone strong like you, please, love me, and the poor commander will also play his part, I left him in the farmhouse on the mountain, he looked dead, but he wasn't, he's been there, growing old, he's waiting for us, come join us, we'll make a nice threesome, I promise. Twilight's fallen, how strange, it was dawn in the mountain valley, and suddenly it's twilight, but Tristano smiles at the woman who's stepped outside the farmhouse, the knife he was holding has turned to a wildflower, she waves for him to come inside, come on, come on, Tristano... Tristano steps through the doorway and reenters the dream he was dreaming the moment before, behind that door he doesn't find the rooms of a rustic farmhouse, there are people dancing in a drawing room, and beyond that room is an elegant garden that seems like the garden of a Tuscan villa, with cypress trees and boxwood hedges, and people holding glasses, and waiters in white jackets, Tristano is back at a *garden party* with the German officer who's now his valet, no longer Marilyn, an older gentleman, face withered, skin peppered with age spots, who whispers a German name that Tristano doesn't recall, the man has a monocle over his right eye and a stiff leg, maybe a false leg, who knows. In his dream, Tristano thinks that many German aristocrats lost a leg in the first world war, and then he thinks that this German might start dancing on the table, but that's from reading books and watching movies, and dreams aren't innocent... instead, with the unsurprised surprise of dreams, the German baron with the monocle starts speaking in English, says *I'm American*, and then he whispers other things lost in the murmuring of the guests, *freedom... freedom...* please, let me introduce you to the other guests, and his voice is icy, metallic, creaking like his false leg... What a nightmare... but it's not a real nightmare, because I'm awake now, so I'm not telling you my dream, I'm telling you something I see, now and then this something will let go of me, like now, I've escaped, but then it sucks me back in as if I'm really living it, look, I'm not telling you my nightmare, it's something real, I'm in the midst of it, must be all those drugs together, and then my head's exploding, just exploding... Tristano, honey... He turned around: Marilyn was at the back of the garden, and she was dressed like a little girl, with bows in her pigtails, she was lying in the grass, her skirts pulled up to her belly, legs spread, behind her was a seaport with the words *freedom harbor* written out, and beside her was some stranger, balding, squat, round-faced, smiling, join us, this pipsqueak muttered, this is the revolution, but

Tristano didn't understand… what's that? This chubby pip-squeak asked if he knew how to shoot a gun, we need sharp guys like you, don't bother with those idiots and their parties, we're using them, they're useful, and the worse they are the better, explain it to your boy, Rosamunda, what kind of a partisan is he, anyway? – join us, Tristano, it's time to kill – haven't you figured that out yet? – explain it to him, Marilyn, tell him it's time to kill… his voice lingering like an echo, kiiiiiiiiiiiiiiillll. Someone tapped his shoulder, a tall man, ugly, with a huge nose and a crooked smile, let me introduce you to the head of state of the sunken republic, Big Nose whispered in Tristano's ear, he has very close contacts who can provide all kinds of services, treat him with the proper respect, he's got more dead enemies on his conscience than there are grapes in a vineyard. Then Big Nose and the decorated military man took him by the elbows and steered him toward the huge barbecue pit blazing on the far side of the garden, gathered around this pit was a group of maybe ten little old men with white eyebrows carrying plates and nib-bling on sausages, the air smelled entirely different in this part of the garden, more of a country fair, a sausage festival, with a tune playing that seemed familiar to Tristano but that he couldn't place, coming from an old gramophone by the braziers. Cloned Mr. Presidents of the future republic, shouted Big Nose, it is my distinct privilege to present to you a great national hero, a man who drove out the invader – celebrate him now, before he kicks you in the ass! The ten little old men started joyfully skip-ping about, tossing their sausages in the air, singing the anthem

along with the gramophone, *si è cinto la testa, si è cinto la testa*!
But at that moment, out from the bush popped a squat bulldog
of a fellow in a double-breasted jacket, who stomped arrogantly
over to Tristano and said, friend, don't listen to the proletarian
revolutionaries, don't listen to these old farts from the retirement
home, listen to me, I'm the one who's going to be in charge, the
founder of the Pippopippi Republic, you want to be appointed
manager of a top-notch program? The squat fellow licked his
lips and out shot a chameleon-like tongue that washed his entire
face clean. I'm your future, my dear partisan, he said, his tone
of voice brooked no reply, I'm the reason you fought in the mountains, if you didn't know it, so listen up, I'm going to tell you one
thing and one thing only because I have a bass dinner waiting
for me that my cook prepared, so here it is: Christ brought too
many people from the East to our door, he was a Bedouin, he
rode along on a donkey just to annoy to us – we're a car-based
civilization…


Ferruccio said if you start looking in the most hidden crev-
ices of society, anywhere you look, you'll find madness. But all
those brave enough to look were mad themselves… Sorry to
cut off Tristano's dream… I didn't get to finish it myself, there
came a point when the dream was interrupted by some guy riding along on a donkey, I think, and then I was really asleep, the
drugs must have worn off, and so did the hallucination, Frau told
me there hadn't been a storm, she's always one for giving out bad

news, she's spent her life giving out bad news, she comes in and says, young sir, the evening storm they predicted last night didn't come, so it's hotter than it was before, but your room's cooler than anywhere else in the house, so you should be content, the nurse is taking two days off, her son has the chickenpox, I was the one who stayed with you last night, and you slept like an angel, not one peep out of you, it's time for your morphine, but I'm not going to give it to you, it's poisoning you, I'm not saying you're not hurting, but your life's been better than mine, and I never complain, you ever hear me complain? Do you?

Writer, you know who Tristano was fighting for? Go on… of course you do, you're just not thinking… one day Tristano realized, just like that, a flash of insight, one of those things… what's that called in literature?… you know, when reality's fixed like concrete, and then, as if by an act of god, there's suddenly a crack, and you can peer into that crack, and you understand… it's like a tiny miracle, am I making myself clear? Well… never mind… Tristano understood who it was he'd struggled for – who it was he'd fought and killed and risked being killed for… and what all the pain and suffering and ideals were for. It was for pippopippi. That's what I call it because that's what Tristano called that thing over there, pippopippi, and it's not just the gadget, I mean the box, the physical object, the empirical evidence, the visible thing. The pippopippi that Tristano understood was some sort of god, some entirely new, unknown god, whose religion was an absence of religion and so devoid of any substance… and this very lack of substance was the source of its extraordinary power, superior to any ity or ism, Christianity, Judaism, Buddhism, Islamism, Shintoism, Taoism, it could participate in all of these and be no one, revealing, then, a nature that was both protein and absolute, not pure spirit, visible and illusory at once, the projection of itself and all things, dreams and desires, everything and nothing, composed of electrons, of energy, but not of molecules… Curiously, Tristano understood this without watching pippopippi, because when you watch it, it isn't it; it's only its hypostasis… Tristano understood the essence of pippopippi one summer night, while standing on the terrace off this room, it was an extremely clear night and he was staring up at the starry sky and thinking about Doctor Ziegler's theories, and while he was looking for the Big Dipper or Orion, he caught sight of a star that was moving, that wasn't a star, because it was moving and too sparkly, so it had to be artificial, and he thought he caught the beep beep of this new star out in sidereal space and it seemed to him that he was catching something in code, and he was hearing… don't think, people, don't think, remember not to think, thinking's hard, it's useless, you started thinking to make a tool from flint and then came the earthenware pot and the shovel and the chamber pot and Zyklon B and the atomic bomb, yep, good job thinking, you must be tired of thinking, just think of me and I'll think of you, so you'll have done your thinking, I'm pippopippi and I'll protect you from thought itself… Tristano looked down over the plain dotted with lights from the houses, then farther, to the light from the city, the smear of yellow reflected in the night sky, and the voice of that artificial star seemed to draw all those lights together, and all those lights together let out a distant roar, like the ground churning from an earthquake, a rumbling, a grumbling all together, a Biblical sound, like something from the Book of Revelations, and this is what they rumbled: pippopippi, we're thinking your thoughts, thank you, pippopippi… Ah, it was a bad dream, and he started having nightmares, now pippopippi's voice began to visit him even during REM, what Doctor Ziegler called deep sleep, and its voice was flute-like or falsetto, a confessor's whisper through the confessional grate: don't think, remember not to think, let me think for you, Tristano, you fought for freedom and freedom's come: it's being liberated from thinking, no longer thinking… real freedom's when you're thought.

Do you know the poem that goes, long shadows over the sea, your smile, my love, and your caresses soon grow resigned, like shadows at night… and then it continues with the horizon, the waves, and all the other clichés? You know that one? Don't tell me you know it… it doesn't exist, no one ever wrote it, and it sounds so ordinary, let's just put it to rest.

…but he wouldn't cry, he mustn't cry, he didn't like crying. And laughing? It's nothing to laugh at, the *ridens* philosopher said, laughing while he spoke… That unfree man was breathless pain that brought on choking rage, and what else could he do but scream madly into the void, cry and cluck in the vineyard, when the midday is silent heat, grinding teeth, and wails of grief, killing even the shrilling of the cicada?… Listen, listen, how did the Abderites diagnose him… you never heard of them? That's what he called them, those doctors putting on their highfalutin doctor airs… a diagnosis with the stamp of the local health department, complete with case history and description, listen now, this was their diagnosis… man gaunt in appearance, long beard, eyes at times cloudy as though affected by choleric humors that render the cornea yellow, swearing under breath not infrequent, normally won't respond to even the most basic questions, as though he is elsewhere, so remains silent during medical session, and still quiet, gets up to leave without turning around, and if he does turn around, makes a bizarre gesture more mocking than any form of salutation, refuses medication that has restored the smile to millions and that the state would supply free of charge, even if he is well-to-do, in the first attempt at psychological examination, patient stated they might as well, quote, stop breaking his balls about his childhood because it was happy, you'd never find one happier, he remembers an anticlerical grandfather who was passionate about astronomy, he remembers his initiation at age fifteen with an unidentified female, one of their farmworkers, a grown woman, and it was marvelous, he says the problem's not up in the mountains but down by the sea, he's insisted on a prescription for laudanum, that we of course didn't prescribe, and he responded to our justified medical refusal with guffaws… This, the diagnosis of the Abderites, rendered scientific, my dear Damagetus, with a certifying stamp… today I think you're my Damagetus, that's what I'll call you today, and you must have read the pages concerning this madness, because that's where Tristano found himself, just like Damagetus writes, he was stuck between laughter and fury, the two extremes that life has to offer us at times, stuck, you might say, between a rock and a hard place, and no fissure between these two extremes, which is where *virtus* would lie, but Tristano had no *virtus*, couldn't find any. He considered the treatment for imbalanced humors in the ancient world, tears or laughter, but neither would do, because his pain was mute, continuous, inarticulate, gnawing at his chest, searching for a voice, for words, like a creature howling deep inside a tunnel… He wasn't inside a tunnel, the tunnel was him, he'd become a tunnel… And one day in the vineyard he saw a toad… and that toad became a dog… or did I mention this already?… patience, now, you can always rewrite it… a yellow toad that became a yellow dog with its head poking up from the ground where it had been buried, its mouth wide open… you could see down its throat, it was suffocating, the toad went glog glog, and then its voice turned into a dog's voice, and now it showed its broken, decaying teeth, boo boo boo, it said, I'm you and you're me, am I making myself clear?… This creature, it was being extremely clear, and

Tristano suddenly understood that this was his brother... no...
his mirror. And the world began to spin. He was pissing, facing
the vineyard, pissing on his shoes, feeling drunk, the way you
do when you suddenly understand something and start feeling
dizzy, sand on sand, what he'd believed, what he'd given for
freedom, a freedom buried up to the neck in sand, thank you,
Tristano, you've really been a good little watch dog, now bark if
you can, and if you can't, then nip at the wind... Tristano looked
that toad in the eye and everything was written there, and he
understood now, but it was too late, the bombs had gone off,
the dead were dead, the murderers were on holiday and the
republican brass band was playing in the piazzas, because it
was June second, and the sacred flag was snapping in the wind,
and officials stood at attention by the flag, like Tristano stood
at attention by the vineyard while pissing on his shoes... He
saluted the toad, at your command, Signor Toad, and the toad
half-dog half-toad let out a sharp cry like sirens probably cry, on
that first sultry day on the plains, a voice from the mountains, a
cool voice blowing down from snowy peaks, a faint song, spill-
ing over layers of time, but sharp still, a voice calling, the olive
falls, no leaves fall, your beauty won't ever, you're like the sea of
waves, go beddy-bye, go beddy-bye, you traitor. Tristano wheeled
around, staggering, sought out the shadow of his room, threw
himself onto the bed, covered his ears, and tried to sleep. Which
as you can imagine, writer, wasn't possible.

Pancuervo! Pancuervo! he started screaming one day. Frau rushed to his study: he seemed to be dozing in his chair, a branch from the cherry tree was coming through the open window beside him. It was the end of May, the cherries were bright red, he leaped to his feet and screamed out the window, at the fields, Pancuervo! Frau stood very still, petrified, he stepped onto the sunny terrace, raced down the stone steps, and started dancing round the cherry tree, grasping the trunk now and then, tugging, as if he wanted to pull the tree up by the roots, kicking his legs high like a wild man of the forest, screaming, cherry pink and apple blossom white!... Frau had followed behind him and stood there, terrified, while he danced crazily and sang these strange words, and she thought he was having some kind of fit, poor Frau, she was petrified, stood absolutely still, even when he raced off to the fields, still screaming, Pancuervooo! Pancuervooo!... It wasn't some kind of fit, it was that he understood, he suddenly understood, a flash of lightning come too late, that it all began in Pancuervo many years before, that there, at the end of the line from his boy exploding, sat Pancuervo, that's where he had to look, Pancuervo... But did Pancuervo really exist?... The train pulled in, then pulled away, but he hadn't climbed on board, he'd stayed put in a remote little station in Castile, staring off at the rolling hills, barren and strange, hills like white elephants.

…I was just drowsing a little and something popped into my head… why are you doing all this? I mean, you put up with my rotten moods, and everything else… in my opinion you're a tricky devil, no offense, and maybe you don't even realize it… well… you're awfully patient… so that phrase popped into my head, tricky devil… don't be offended, I'm a jerk, no, I'm a jailed jerk, blame it on this gangrene that's eating me alive, I think it's got my balls by now, do me a favor, get me that menthol talcum powder on the dresser… sorry to be so intimate, but I've been telling you such private things, we're pretty close at this point… I notice you come rushing in at the ring-a-ling of my bell, no matter what time it is, even if it's just to hear me say something mean to you, like right now… So, I guess Tristano's life really must matter to you, huh?

The Abderites insisted that Tristano was raving mad, and I told you he was crazy, too, but the truth is, he just arrived too early… early arrivals always seem crazy, they're fated to be Cassandras, they might just be little nothing Cassandras, but nothing Creons are still scared of them, that's why they invented asylums, places to stuff those harmless Cassandras, while the dangerous people are on the outside, and they're the ones in charge… You know what's going to happen, writer?… I'll tell you what Tristano thought after he figured out pippopippi's true nature, because now it's all coming to pass… pippopippi, with the solemn goal of obliterating from the mind any thought that might be harmful to him, to pippopippi, will slowly expunge all images carrying even the slightest trace of thought from all his glass boxes, until you're all completely weaned, and anything with any sign of meaning will have completely disappeared, because the image itself, even the most paltry, wretched, repulsive image – like the ones they dish up to you every night – can lead to a thought, and thoughts are dangerous… and so you all will simply stare at the light, at the trembling electric lines, the crackling dots of light, where you'll lose your thoughts, and the shipwreck will be sweet for you in that shimmering… a modern nirvana?, maybe the fateful mu, finally attained, that Buddhism speaks of. That's what awaits you tomorrow, writer, because after all, as Scarlett said, tomorrow is another day, I can see you all there, at night, gathered in your carpeted caves, fixated on your electric fire, all of you together murmuring muuuu… and on the hearth I lay my war cross, that piece of junk, because he shall be the lord your god, and you shall have no other gods before him… not that the electric fires in other countries will be so different from yours, to each according to his due… I say your country because mine's almost gone… I'm already more there than here, my feet practically swinging in the air, I'm stateless, I don't belong to anyone, my passport's useless for the customs I have to get through, and there's no one who can grab hold of my feet and pull me down from the orange tree, like Tristano did for his Daphne, that I can assure you.

...as I was saying, letters started arriving. No – voices – they arrived in the form of voices, even if he saw them as written, he could read each and every one of them written in the air, all with different handwriting, because each voice had its own handwriting, the timbre of the writing, each had its own tone, its own inflection, the color of the voice sending the letter. Doctor Ziegler had told him this sort of thing sometimes happened... sounds turned to colors, a type of aura... even the ink varied in color, with all shades of the color spectrum, mostly black, but also white on black sometimes, and yellows, and oranges like a summer sunset... reds... a few blues... a great many greens, all kinds of green, bottle-green, flag-green, Verona-green, and especially blister-green verging on brownish yellow. That green entered his auricle like a hiss, a green carried by the sound of sssssssssss... hissing, snaking letters, the green whistling in his ears turning magically bitter on his tongue, like chewing on a thistle. He called that green bitter-green. And he received numerous letters every day, ten, twenty, more, even at night, he'd finally fall asleep, after a great deal of effort, he might not even dream, he'd turn off like a radio turned off, no reception... actually he fooled himself into thinking he'd shut off all contact, over and out, but no, he might be over but he wasn't out... the thing would start with a sizzle, I'm not sure how to describe it, like when you twist the radio dial and there's a crackling, and he'd wake up, hoist his head off the pillows, frozen in the dark room, a letter was arriving, that strange mailman was ringing, the doorbell insisting, sizzling in the dark, as though they'd laid his ear on a red-hot grill, shssss shssss shssss, and they weren't all written in black or bitter-green ink, maybe some were in blue, even a sky blue, a blur of childhood and lost memories… Dear Ninototo, you scratched Ninototo Ninototo all over the walls of the stable with a piece of coal, and I found that amusing, because no one taught you how to write, so you learned it on your own, but this morning, I found this same writing on the wall to the farm, and along with it, words I never heard you say, and I had to call Amilcare, and it took two buckets of lime to cover all that writing, all those words, my dear boy, you mustn't write these things, because they shock peasants like Amilcare, on Sundays they go to mass, and the priest will scold them if they say these words, and finding them written here has an impact, these peasants are respectful, they believe in god, and we must let them believe in god, so you may only say these words to Nonno when we're together, otherwise Nonno won't take you to the town fair again for the San Giovanni Festival, like we did last year, is that clear, Ninototo?… His grandfather's voice was written in blue. His grandfather kept a red shirt hanging in his wardrobe because he'd been in Garibaldi's army, and there was a saber leaning against the red shirt that Ninototo saw on Saturday afternoons when he was allowed in his grandfather's room. But even with that red shirt, his grandfather's voice was sky-blue and Tristano, head hoisted off the pillows, completely awake at this point, frightened, would clearly see that blue voice in the dark. Nonno, he'd say into the darkness, why'd you wake me? – I was just falling asleep, I can barely sleep these days, listen,

Nonno, that was so long ago, I don't remember anymore, so much time has passed, Nonno, I'm as old as you – no, older – please, Nonno, rest in peace and let me rest, too, but what's gotten into you, sending me a letter just now, I worked so hard to fall asleep, you know, I'm all alone now, I don't have anyone anymore, that boy I loved like a son brought death with him… so gentle, so quiet, how's that even possible?… Nonno, what I did back then was wrong, I know why you're scolding me, but are you trying to tell me what I did as a grownup was wrong, too, is that why you're writing me, Nonno?

…Another letter, hard to define the color, maybe colorless. My darling Clark, that's what I'll call you from now on, since no one knows your name here, you've given out two or three, but only the commander knows your real name, I'm going to call you Clark because with that wisp of hair on your forehead and that little ironic smile, you resemble an actor from my country that I really like, but I like you even more, and I like it when you wrap your strong arms around me at night, but tonight we can't, my darling Clark, I know you're going down to the valley with the squad they've given you, I'm going down with the Gesso squad, you're headed to the eastern versant, I'm headed to the western versant, the commander finally ordered me into action, and this is why they had me parachute into these mountains, he'll stay here by himself, but he's got nothing to worry about, the Savoy soldiers make good guards, and tomorrow night

I'll be back with you in your shelter, I promise, I think after this military action you'll have to obey me and stop calling me Rosamunda, I don't like it when you call me that, my name's Marilyn, and you, Clark, what's your name, won't you tell me?... Another: bitter-green. Tristano, you're awful, what you're suggesting's obscene, it was a paradoxical affair, not tied to my real life, my heart was always so full of this frustrated love for you, there was very little room for a man in my life, and that paradoxical situation was, paradoxically, the only one that worked for me... I wasn't the one who betrayed you in the mountains, you wanted to believe that – and you know why, too – you know you needed to think that someone else was doing the betraying... Another: a rich color. Dear comrade, I'm not writing to you as commander, I'm writing to you as a comrade, if it's all right to call you that even if you might not entirely sympathize with the deeper meaning of the word. I really appreciate your position and how honest you've been with me about your political views, I don't want you to think that I consider you a bourgeois intellectual as you've accused me, and I also don't want you to think of me as a diehard proletarian-lover, which is how you put it, and which didn't offend me in the least, you should know this, because I value your ideas just as I hope you value mine, you're brave and I respect you as a man and as a combatant, when all this is over, we'll sit down and calmly discuss our ideas; for now, let's just stick to firing at the enemy, and not at each other... Another: yellow. Tristano, I'm beginning to understand that no one wants to take responsibility for anything in your country, as if everything that happened, what we came to rid you of, was no one's fault, and this allowed some to flirt with communist countries, as if any kind of totalitarianism was good, no matter what, me, I'm staying in Spain for now, I don't have the heart to go back to Cincinnati, *Spain's different*, really, and the ghost of old Ernest surrounds me here, is my amulet... but why did you decide to stay behind at that small train depot in the middle of nowhere, why didn't you come with me, was it because you were afraid to understand? Another: black, in black vestments. Tristano, I entrusted him to you, and you didn't know how to protect him, and you're not capable of cutting off her head, the head of Medusa who hypnotized him, you're the same coward you were back then.


...Because he had a mirror, Perseus managed to cut off the head of Medusa, who turned people to stone with her stare, and when he held up his trophy by the snake hair, he was able to free Andromeda from the sea monster, and then he married her... The principal star in the Perseus constellation is Algenib, or Mirfak... Arabic names... the Arabs were such great navigators, always sailing the seas and studying the stars... In Arabic, Algenib means keep to the right, and this is the brightest star, easily seen with the naked eye... thousands of times brighter than the sun, but the most well-known star is Algol, which means the demon's head, apparently sailors found this star the most useful, who knows why... the Perseids are shooting stars that originate in the Perseus constellation, astronomers say they're the remains of lasting comets, comets that have lasted god knows how long, you can see them around the tenth of August, maybe if you take a peek out the window, you'll get to see them, I always did, it was like an appointment, every August tenth, but it must be long past August tenth by now, lying here, I've lost track.

I landed on this island late in the day. From the ferry, I watched the harbor approaching, and the small white town perched around the Venetian-style castle, and I thought, maybe he's here. And I wandered narrow lanes that led to the tower, carrying my suitcase that every day grew lighter, and up every step I'd repeat to myself, maybe he's here. In the small square below the castle, a terrace overlooking the harbor, there's a cheap restaurant with old iron tables along a low wall, two flower beds with two olive trees, and bright red geraniums in rectangular pots. Old men sit on the wall and talk quietly, children run around a marble bust of a mustached captain, a hero in the Balkan Wars of the twenties. I sat down at a small table, set my suitcase on the ground, smoothed my skirt, and ordered a typical island dish, rabbit and onions, that smelled of cinnamon. The first tourists show up in early June. Night was falling, a clear night, the cobalt sky going bright purple, then darker, to indigo. Out on the water, the lights glimmered from the villages of Paros, which seemed only a few short steps away. Yesterday I met a doctor on Paros. He's from the South, I believe from our Crete, though I didn't ask. He's short and stocky, with a veined nose. I was watching the horizon and he asked if I was watching the horizon. I'm watching the horizon, I answered. The only line that breaks the horizon, he said, is a rainbow. An optical trick, pure illusion. And we talked about illusions, and though I didn't want to, I spoke of you, I brought up your name without even trying, and he told me he met you once because he'd sutured your veins after you slit your wrists. I didn't know, and I was moved, and I thought I'd find a bit of you in him, because he'd known your blood. So I went back with him to his hotel, the Thalassa, on the boardwalk, it was dingy, full of the sort of middle-class foreigners who spend their vacations in Greece and detest the Greeks. But he wasn't like them, he was kind, shy when he undressed, and his member was small, slightly twisted, like those terracotta satyr statues in the Athens museum. And it wasn't so much that he wanted a woman as a few comforting words, because he was unhappy, and I pretended to comfort him, for pity's sake. I looked for you, my love, for every speck of you dispersed in the universe. I gathered what I could, from the ground, the air, the sea, the glances and gestures of others. I even looked for you in the kouroi on a far-off mountain of one of these islands, because you told me once that you sat on a kouros's lap. It wasn't easy getting up there. The bus left me in Sypouros, if that's what this unknown village is even called, since it's not on any map, and then I had to do the last three kilometers on foot, I trudged up the winding dirt road, which further on, led to a valley of cypresses and olive trees. There was an old shepherd by the road, and I said the only word to him that mattered: kouros. And his eyes shone with a light of complicity as though he understood, as though he knew who I was and who I was looking for, that I was looking for you, and without a word, he pointed to a path, and I gathered up his guiding gesture and that brief light shining in his eyes, and I put them in my pocket, look, they're right here, I could lay them out on this little patio table where I'm dining, they're two more chips of the crumbled fresco I'm desperately gathering, trying to put you back together, along with the smell of that man I spent the night with and the rainbow on the horizon and this pale blue sea that makes me feel so anxious. And above them all is the barred window I discovered on Santorini, the one with a grapevine climbing the bars, which looks out over the vast sea and a small public square. The sea was endless kilometers, and the small square a few meters across, and I recalled some poems about the sea and about squares, a sea of shimmering tiles that I saw from a cemetery with you, and a small square and the people living there who'd seen your face, and I looked for you in the shimmering of that sea because you'd seen it, and in the eyes of the shopkeeper, the pharmacist, the little old man who sold iced coffee in that small square, because they'd seen you. And I put these things in my pocket, too, in this pocket that's myself and my eyes. A priest stepped onto the church square. He was sweating in his black robes and reciting a Byzantine liturgy and the kyrie was colored by you. On the horizon, a boat leaves a trail of white foam over the blue. Is that you as well? Perhaps. I might put it in my pocket. But in the meantime a foreigner, an early tourist – early for the season, but practically old herself – is on a payphone by the sea that's open to the wind and anyone passing by, and she's saying, *Here the weather is wonderful. I will remain very well.* And these are your words, I recognize them even in another language, though of course we know this is just a tourist's attempt at translating something you've already said into English. Spring has passed for us, my dearest friend, my dearest love. And autumn's come, with its yellowing leaves. No – it's the dead of winter in this untimely summer cooled by a breeze on this terrace overlooking Naxos Port. Windows, that's what we need, a wise old man in a distant country once told me, the vastness of reality is incomprehensible, and to understand it, we must lock a rectangle around it, geometry is opposed to chaos, that's why men invented windows that are geometrical, and every structure assumes right angles. And is our life subject to right angles as well? You know, those difficult routes, composed of segments that we all must get through just to reach our death. Perhaps, but if a woman like me sits thinking on an open terrace by the Aegean Sea on a night like this, she understands that everything we think and live and have lived and imagine and long for, that all of this can't be governed by geometry. And that windows are only a timid geometric form for men afraid of the circular gaze, where everything beyond the window frame might enter, senseless and irreparable, like Thales gazing at the stars. Everything I collected of you, crumbs, dust, fragments, traces, guesses, intonations left behind in others' voices, grains of sand, a conch, your past that I imagined, our supposed future, what I wanted from you, what you promised me, my childhood dreams, the love I felt for my father as a child, some silly poems from my youth, a poppy along a dusty road – that went into my pocket, too, you understand? The corolla of a poppy, like the poppies I'd collect in May, when I drove up into the hills in my Volkswagen, while you stayed home, consumed with your projects, the complicated recipes your mother left you, scribbled in French in a little black book, and I'd gather poppies for you, and you didn't understand. I don't know if you planted your seed in me, or if it was the other way around. Each of us is alone, with no transmission of future flesh, and most of all I have no one to gather up my anguish. All of them, I've wandered all these islands, all of them, searching for you. And this is the last, just as I'm the last. After me, no more. And who besides me would look for you? I won't betray you, cut the thread. Not even knowing where your body lies. You surrendered to your Minos, whom you thought you'd tricked, but who swallowed you instead. And so I read epigraphs in every cemetery I can find, searching for your beloved name, where I might cry for you at least. Two times you betrayed me, the second, when you hid your body. And now here I sit at this table on a terrace, staring out to sea, eating rabbit seasoned with cinnamon. A lazy old Greek is singing an ancient song for coins. There are cats, children, two British tourists my age talking about Virginia Woolf, and a lighthouse in the distance that they don't even see. I made you leave the labyrinth that you forced me into, but for me there's no exit, not even one that's final. Because my life is over, and everything is slipping past, with no chance for a connection that will lead me back to myself or to the cosmos. I'm here, the breeze caresses my hair, and I'm groping in the dark, because I've lost my thread, Theseus, the one I gave you…

You like it? I thought about it all night, rewrote it in my head, word for word, but I'm sure you'll improve it once you write it down; make it poignant, if you can… I'm not much good at heartbreak, but that's exactly what this calls for, because this is a letter that truly came out of nowhere… Who wrote that letter to Tristano, and from what depths did it emerge, like a relentless sea-bass pushing up in time from the bottom of the ocean until one day it breaks the surface of the water? Was she still living, that woman searching for his grave? – and why – to dig her own beside it? Daphne was no longer there, but her voice remained, so her search for him remained as well. Can we survive ourselves? Who can say… Eyes wide-open in the dog days of August, with words from a letter but no letter in his hand, the air thick with viscous remorse, like ammoniac gas leaking from a punctured pipe, Tristano stood there, frozen in the blinding midday sun, naked as the day he was born, as he'd fled from the house, fled from voices invoking spirits that were invoking him… his hanging, flaccid member, a useless compass needle, indicating a non-cardinal point that he knew to be the ground, and more than the ground, the bottom, and more than the bottom, the pit, and eternity... and the slight kiss of light on his body turned to shadow, blinding shadow that swallowed all... He raised his arms, groping, and he felt he inhabited nothing, was made of nothing, too. Was he already dead? Who could say, who could say... No one can say, writer, I'm the only one who knows, and maybe I don't know, either, because you don't just die on the outside, you die on the inside even more.

I'll be honest, before you came I thought I'd tell you everything about Mavri Elià, no one's ever mentioned her, and luckily, you ignored her in your book as well... I told myself that I'd make things right again. How foolish, as if things could be made right in this life... but I don't feel like it anymore, Mavri Elià is Tristano's and his alone, why should I give her to you, you don't deserve her... at most, I'll give you a few of the essential details, limit myself to the so-called facts. But what do facts mean?... the facts... let's say this... the facts... when she disappeared, for instance... when she passed away, like someone might say who uses expressions like, it is my obligation to, and, my condolences. So stupid, people don't die, it is my obligation to be precise, they're only under a spell... a writer you must be familiar with said we're under the spell of those who love us – I mean those who really really love us – and we wind up floating off the ground, like balloons, though no one sees, the only ones who see are those who love us, those who really really love us, and they rise up on tiptoe, give a little hop, just a bounce, and grab hold of our legs, which at this point have turned to air, and they pull us down, keep hold of us, otherwise we'd start flying again, rising again, but they link their arm in ours, holding us down, down with them, as if nothing had occurred, as we do with certain pretenses in our life, a matter of social convention, so we won't look bad in front of the shopkeeper or the tobacco-store owner who's known you forever and might say, but look at that strange guy arm-in-arm with his wife who's floating right off the ground… and that's what happened to him, to Tristano, it was Sunday, and even if it wasn't, make it Sunday, because I've decided that everything important to Tristano happened on a Sunday, and if you write it this way in your book, what you write will become true, because when things are written down they become true… and it was August, because I've decided all the important things in Tristano's life happened on a Sunday in August, and if you write it this way, then it will become true as well, you'll see… he wandered around empty Plaka and thought about how sad she looked at times, and about some sad evenings at Malafrasca, Daphne, pensive, staring out the open windows toward the plains, the gas lamps, and her saying in her Crete accent, Tristano, if there's one thing I want, it's not to be buried out there when I die, in that cemetery covered by fog, take me home and have me cremated, and scatter my ashes in my sea, around my Aegean islands, but nothing dramatic, please, something simple, just wander here and there, go from one island to the next, borrow a little fishing boat, take it a little ways out from shore, not too far, at Sifnos, Naxos, Paros, and throw a pinch here, a pinch there, and also, please lie naked in the bottom of the boat, like when we made those trips because you got it into your head to fish for gambusinen, but you never did fish for them, and we'd wind up making love, the boat rocking crazily and you shouting, shipwrecked once more!... Tristano stopped at the men's shop in Plaka, she was lying in the Byzantine chapel nearby, it was so hot... and he thought the shopkeeper might find a way to get her back because he'd known her since she was a girl, but the shopkeeper didn't remember her, then Tristano went to the snack kiosk and asked the little man if he remembered a woman who bought candies there as a girl, her name's Daphne, Phine, her friends always called her Phine, she's lying in a coffin in the chapel close by, on the square, if you remember her, could you give her back to me? I've heard about these magic spells, and I'm trying... But the little man at the kiosk didn't remember Daphne, sorry, he said, but Greece is filled with Daphnes... and then Tristano turned to the legless woman selling violets, and the legless woman selling violets remembered her at once, of course, of course, she said, that girl with eyes like two black olives, it was a long time ago, but I remember her very well, look, she hasn't just vanished into thin air, she's right there beside you, up by that orange tree, just grab her legs and pull her down... Spells are strange, writer, because just like that, Tristano swung round and there was Mavri Elià floating by an orange tree, and he told her, how silly, I'm old and must be going blind, you were right there behind me and I didn't even notice, thank god for the lady selling violets who made me see you were only under a spell… Thank you, ma'am, he said to the legless woman selling violets, and he pulled Daphne down from the tree and they started strolling around Plaka, but it wasn't as he thought, it was a winter day, and Daphne was saying, come inside the door, they're shooting – it's dangerous – and you've killed a German officer.

Ferruccio said that lesser organisms have greater vitality than those that are more evolved. That's the theory of someone who died young, people who think like that have to die young, just to be consistent… I'd tell you a story, a nice little tidbit, something no one really suspects, but I'm tired now, it must be getting late, I need to sleep… I'll say it briefly, and you'll have to do some embellishing, because it's not all that exciting… but right now I really need to sleep, I can't hold out any longer. Tomorrow, please come early, at dawn even, I'll be awake then, there's not much time left, I want to die before the end of August, and September's knocking at the door, I can hear it.

I realize we're at the end now, I'm telling you this because tonight I was thinking of entering my circle… I mean, I've already been trotting around in here a little while… funny verb, to trot, for someone with a leg in this condition, can't you just see it?… I can – try to picture it – some scrawny old guy, completely naked, just a sheet around him, dragging his chewed-up leg, hopping around in an empty space, making a circle… thinking about it, you want to cheer him on… get in there, go on, decide already, you can do it!… There's something I was thinking I wouldn't tell you, I've resisted up to now, I was thinking to myself that all in all, it didn't really add anything, anyway, and then I told myself that it's not like it does much for Tristano's character… just the opposite… and it feels like I've already ruined your character a bit… but ruined isn't the right word… troubles… you know, a writer invents a character and purifies him somehow… I'm not being very clear here, it's not that the writer purifies his character, it's that whatever this character is, even if the author gives his character a human life – and people's lives are filled with troubles, man's a cruel animal – it's still a life on paper, and on paper, troubles don't stink… but if someone tells you certain things that he's actually lived, and more than that, if he tells you these things in the flesh, right next to you, and he's breathing and maybe his flesh isn't in the best of shape, either, then those troubles he's telling you are less aseptic, am I making myself clear?… But, when someone's reaching the end… in short, I thought that thanks to you, these troubles will turn to paper, and so you'll render them more abstract. But troubles aren't… who knows… at times it's so hard to tell the difference between cruelty and justice… killing… or murdering… Tristano was a pacifist, you know this from that interview a long time ago, before he made himself disappear, and he was especially opposed to the death penalty, that obtuse,

bureaucratic, state-provided death on officially stamped paper…
sure, but this is a matter of principle and would be worth something in a perfect world, and if you follow this principle to the extreme, then you need to go embrace that Chilean general who murdered thousands in the stadiums, go on, give him a hug and tell him about loving his fellow man, maybe you'll wind up friends… Unfortunately, the world's not like Tolstoy imagined, where you can convince a murderer through love and forgiveness… it would be beautiful, this utopia. Hitler promised that Nazism would reign a thousand years in Europe, you think we should allow it in the name of brotherly love?… Our principles rule out homicide, but killing a tyrant – the Beast – who'd devour our principles, this doesn't contradict our principles…
Anyway, I'll leave that dilemma to you, it doesn't concern me anymore… I'll be brief, I don't feel like going into too much detail, and really, it's not necessary for the story, all you need to know is that Tristano wasn't alone and that Taddeo was driving. A detail: Tristano wasn't young anymore, no, he was old and needed some company… and Taddeo was also rather old, but he was the company Tristano wanted… No, listen, I've changed my mind, I'm only going to give you the details of the story, that's what I want, I'm leaving out the essential part, you'll figure that out on your own… meaning, where Tristano learned to unravel the knot, how he found the exact right spot, and who helped him in his search… that doesn't matter. Taddeo was driving the car and Tristano was humming a little nursery rhyme, *ahi luna luna luna el niño la mira mira el niño la está mirando…*

There's a gypsy legend that the full moon steals children, the child she stole from him was no longer a child but was still a child to him... Proserpina covers the dead with white sheets, luna luna luna lead the way... the road was dusty white with low shrubs on either side, and it was whiter still in the head-lights... Tristano had already written a postcard to Rosamunda but hadn't mailed it yet, it was still in the glove compartment... everyone had left that small town, it had become a tourist village, said the *carabinero* who gave him directions, but a specific kind of tourist village, *d'élite*, since those living there already were cultural tourists, that's what he'd called them, a thoughtful com-munity, everyone quiet, reflective, not like those young people going to discos or throwing parties with loud music and every-body getting drunk, and we'll have to break them up... And the house was truly elegant as seen from the outside, an old country house remodeled by an intelligent architect, the kind that restores and doesn't ruin the landscape... And its tenant, too, was an elegant gentleman, friendly, and he welcomed them in a friendly manner; for that matter, they came as friends, but I'm not saying how that happened, how they managed to get them-selves welcomed as friends, because that's not a detail... and how things unfolded exactly isn't a detail at all, after they took a seat on those beautiful sofas draped with traditional Castilian shawls, and that pleasant gentleman offered them a first-rate brandy, aged Carlos Primero, this detail's worth emphasizing, because brandy aids in digestion, another important detail, because they'd had an extravagant dinner, he and Taddeo, an important detail, not just for the gazpacho and the roasted *angulas*, which Taddeo had never tried before, but because if it was after dinner, it was night and rather late… A brandy Taddeo liked so well that he accepted a second, and then a third, and while he was drinking his third glass he said – another detail – that he really needed it that evening, something to put some fire in his veins… And now we've arrived at the essential part, what I'll spare you, like I promised… I'd just like to add one more detail, that before this essential part, Tristano set a photo on the table of a boy in a wicker chair under a pergola, a jug of water in front of him and he was holding a book, you could tell it was summer, and the boy had straight, dark hair, and looked happy, his smile spoke of going out to meet the world… And he showed that photo and said… he said… I don't remember, writer, I swear, I couldn't tell you the exact words, but since it's not a detail, I'll just give you the basic gist, you can assume he said he was showing the gentleman that photo because he wanted to emphasize that this boy was his son and that he loved him very much… And at this point, that pleasant gentleman understood everything and became far from pleasant, as you might imagine, and Tristano didn't just stop there, now he wanted to know where this man, this pleasant gentleman, had gotten his orders… which organizations, and whose, meaning, were they overseas or homegrown? And if it was something national, were these men who'd strayed from the right path, or those who'd found the right way? But these are details I'll let you decide on, writer, as to the rest, if you have the patience for it, there's a dossier, thousands of pages' worth, sitting in the archives of our republic's parliament… they're the records of a committee with an unusual name, no other country in Europe has such a committee, we alone can brag of reaching such heights, of our parliamentary committee for mass murder, with its records available to all citizens, if you ever find the time, go take a look, I'm happy to leave all that to you, just like I'm happy to leave you this century… And when the snakes on Medusa's head finally went limp, the two men stepped out into the night, Taddeo got back behind the wheel, there was a beautiful full moon, *luna luna luna el niño la mira mira el niño la está mirando*, and as they drove past a church on a small square, Tristano noticed a mailbox attached to the side of the bell tower, and it seemed like the most fitting mailbox for the postcard he'd written to Rosamunda, *Miss Marilyn-Rosamunda*, celestial Pancuervo, Cosmos. That was the address… an address no postman in this world could trace, but Tristano preferred it that way, he felt as though a weight had been lifted… *In dreams begins responsibility*, I did what you asked me to in a dream. Farewell, Tristano.

In the distance, you could make out fires on the mountains, maybe shepherds. Night was falling, a feeble purple tingeing the strip of land blue, and a word came to him that he hadn't thought of in years, bluing, that blue liquid housekeepers added to the wash… and now the road ran straight toward the mountain, a cluster of lights on the slope, a village, perhaps, no, not

Thebes, Ghiannis said, though Thebes is just a village now, but we've already passed it and you didn't notice, it's just some little town, but now we'll be rounding a lot of curves, we're climbing toward Parnassus, which is only a hill in literature but is really a massive mountain, maybe we'll stop and eat in Arachova... And then Ghiannis started talking about the Crimean War, who knows why, and Tristano recalled his elementary-school teacher who'd loved him, and his schoolbook primer, and on that Parnassus of defunct muses, faceless faces appeared in the night, General La Marmora and his *bersaglieri*, and most of all, a voice singing, I had a pony all dappled gray... But the moon was an icy disc, the road empty; a stray dog by the side of the road seemed to be waiting for someone, straining its neck, head tilted upward, perhaps the creature was howling... And with that image there came another voice, one of those voices that had settled inside him, or maybe it was always the same voice, just different tones, and it was singing a dirge like a lullaby... Antheos, he said, if you know that poem "Voices," then recite it for me in the Greek, would you? My name's not Antheos, Ghiannis said, it's Ghiannis. Do it anyway, Tristano said, you sound just like a friend I had in Plaka many years ago, but I called him Marios, at times we hear them talking in our dreams, at times in thought they echo through the brain... They started up the mountain, the olive grove of Delphi stretched out below, they stopped beside the omphalòs... he looked up. The sky hung low, a blanket of dripping fog, Tristano stroked the curving surface of the stone and then started up toward the temple of Apollo. A little man in raggedy clothes was sitting under the columns of Athena's Sanctuary, trying to keep out of the rain, he had a buzuki on his lap and when he saw Tristano, he started plucking the strings. Tristano gave him a coin and the man began to sing softly, something old, maybe, but he barely even knew the chorus, *tram to teleutaio*, then a dedah dedah… a sad folk song… He asked the man to sing it more clearly, but he didn't understand… *Essùrossa ki arghìsame, ma osso ke na fteo, perpàta na prolàvume, to tram to teleutaio*… I got drunk, we were late, a mistake, but let's grab the last tram, dedah dedah, ring the bell tonight, dedah dedah… it's the last tram… He asked Ghiannis to wait for him, and he started up toward the temple of Apollo, careful to keep his footing on the wet paving stones. He laid his hand on a lopped-off column and made a sign, he'd read somewhere that this was how you called the oracle. He squatted in the rain and lit a cigarette… Not even the shadow of a Pythia – of course not – they hadn't existed for centuries. You idiot, he told himself, you came all this way, you just needed to really concentrate, a nice cozy headache and the Pythia would have come calling… The rain was falling harder, he got to his feet and made his way down slowly in the dark. Far off, on the horizon, he could see the lights on the coast, Galaxidi… a line of trembling lights, yellow, only one was white, strange, that one white light in a line of yellow, Tristano concentrated on that light and it started coming closer, rushing toward him, plowing into him like a meteor, and then he was in a cold, deserted square, a Nazi officer lying at his feet, he stood there, staring in amazement at his rifle, and a girl was pushing open a large front door, gesturing for him to come inside… But is this the riddle I came to solve, he murmured, this past is already clear to me… I know, the cypress answered, this isn't the past you came for… you came to hear your real past told in my voice, because you don't have the courage for it yourself, so you're leaving it to me, predictor of the future, to predict what's already been and won't ever change… so listen… one day, many years ago, you'll find yourself in the woods, in the mountains, on a pale, cold dawn, and you'll be hiding behind a rock and clutching a submachine gun, waiting for your enemies to leave a ruined farmhouse… you'll be impatient, trembling because you're cold and frightened, because what you need to do is critical, the fate of all your comrades, of the ideals you're fighting for, they're in your hands… and finally those enemies will leave the farmhouse, and you'll fire your precise blasts, and kill them all… now that mountain clearing is dead silent, and you get to your feet, triumphant, you're the new squad commander, a hero, you've killed them all and even avenged the old commander's slaughter… but then, something unexpected – your temples are pounding, you're freezing cold – a woman has stepped outside the farmhouse, her hair tousled as though she's been asleep, her eyes wide, astonished, terrified… she sees you, she's standing in the clearing, surrounded by dead soldiers, she looks like a statue, and she's screaming at you, traitor! – spy – traitor!… You'd like to go meet her, tell her he was only an old commander and that it was for one person and one person only that you killed them all… but you don't say a word, as if your thoughts freeze in the air and can't find a voice... how's it possible?... she was supposed to be on a mission tonight in the valley, but... she was here... now you point your gun at her, she's in your sights, one round and you'll be vindicated and the one witness to what really happened will disappear, and you will be a perfect hero... But you won't fire, the Pythia knows this, and so do you... Pilgrim, did you know she spent her nights at that farmhouse? Is that why you became a spy? Or was it because you really wanted to slaughter a German platoon? Or was it because that commander fighting a common enemy believed in a different future than you, and so that made him your enemy as well?... Your life holds three possibilities, pilgrim, but the Pythia can't know what they are: she can predict what's going to happen, but not the will behind it, because Oracles might know what happens outside a man, but they can't read his thoughts.


...But instead, the world's composed of acts, actions... concrete things that then are gone, because, writer, an action takes place, it occurs... and occurs only in that one precise moment, then disappears, is no longer there; it was. For an action to remain, it needs words, which continue to make it be, they bear witness. *Verba volant* isn't true. *Verba manent*. All that remains of what we are and what we were are the words we've said, the words you're writing down now, writer, and not what I did in that given place and that given time. Words remain... my words... and above all, yours... words that bear witness. The word is not at the beginning, writer; it's at the end. But who bears witness for the witness? Here's the point: no one bears witness for the witness… Happy, unhappy, that's not the problem, you know, what I'm consoled by, writer, is that in the great summation of things, in your odious summation filled with figures, I don't figure in, I'm not a single unit among the others, I haven't been counted into the total, okay, you wanted me to be even and I was odd, I screwed up your calculations… That's my poem for Monday, or Tuesday… I've forgotten Sunday's – I didn't like it – so take this as my gift to you instead.

…But in spite of what I was saying earlier, I have an advantage over you, my friend: I am voice; yours is only writing, mine is voice… writing's deaf… these sounds you're hearing in the air will die on the page, writing fixes them, kills them, like a fossil crystallized in quartz… writing is a fossilized voice, no longer living, its spirit, once waves vibrating in space, has disappeared… in a little while my voice will be gone, and your writing will remain… sure, you can record my voice, but it will be dead, it will always be the same words, unchanging, with no volition, into infinity, not a voice, a facsimile of a voice… while what I'm saying to you, even if I have to force myself with my cracked vocal cords that croak and wheeze, the words I say are alive, because they're my breath, until… a voice is breath, writer, listen now, do you hear it, how the cicada's cry shatters the oppressive silence? And the suffocating breathing of the August countryside… do you hear it?… the countryside is breathing like you and me, like everything around us breathes, this globe turning in space, we as we turn on it, and the space we turn in, and the universe that space turns in, and the universes the universe turns in… but stop thinking about the rotation of the earth, think about my head, I've got a splitting headache, right now, as I reach the end, headaches are diehard, harder than we are, see if you can find me something on the dresser, any kind of pill… and god, too, if there is one, god breathes… imagine the lungs he must have… cosmic, I'd say, with monstrous alveoli opening and closing like jaws, measureless breath, but he is breathing… today is the last day for me, or the second to last, I can't be any more precise, but trust me when I say my breathing's at an end, I can hear it, and so's my voice, this voice that's told you a life as best it could, sorry, I'd like to have done a better job, but you probably understand… you don't tell a life, like I already said, you live a life, and while you're living it, it's already lost, has slipped away… so what you've heard is a resurrected time, but it's not the time of that living breath, that breath can't be repeated, all you can do is tell it, like a gramophone… Besides, look, I haven't told you anything new, I've told you an ancient story, History's told this story a thousand times over, poor thing, just like us, we men, History doesn't have many choices, someone had to say it… so someone, always meaning well, has to sacrifice himself… our story started with Judas, and look at our contempt for him, we should reflect more on the sacrifice he made, it's not that easy making a choice, even if you mean well, it was the ultimate choice, the choice of choices, he deserves some rehabilitation, since I'm asking you to rehabilitate a few folks today... there's a colleague of yours from Argentina who's confronted this riddle like few others, I've read him over and over... just incredible... but he makes a theorem of it, maybe he knew little about life and more about its apparatus, what we call paradigms... But when you dig under paradigms you often find shit, and that's hard to solve, there's no solution to shit... You talk about a hero and maybe you find shit... so what do you do – build a statue? Why not? – printed words have the same function, in the end, they're a future memory, like a statue, memory and oblivion at the same time, because someday the first will be swallowed by the second... but if it were only oblivion it would already be quite a lot, because before that there'd be memory, which they say refers to reality, but I'm afraid that words are only under the delusion of grabbing hold of reality... in my view they only describe the apparatus of reality, so we're back to the paradigm... but underneath, is life... teeming life, like when you lift a stone and find an ant nest, ants fleeing in every direction... we call this an ant nest, and everyone understands what we mean by this, but an ant nest is composed of ants, and all the ants have fled. So what do you have left? A hole. Dig, though, go ahead and dig.


Who knows how much they'll wind up hating you for telling my story... especially in this country where you happen to live... and in this century you're moving into. You know, if there's someone everyday judases – who betray just to betray – absolutely hate, it's the real Judas, who betrayed out of loyalty... but don't you pay any attention, you've had the privilege of hearing Tristano's voice, his living voice, as they say, and no one's going to hear it anymore, because it'll be dead. And now, Tristano's truly tired, he's out of breath, listen, he must want to sleep, but not just a quick nap from an injection, a long sleep, the kind of sleep that compensates for all the effort of living... It's time now for his eyelids to lower, for a darkness to spread inside that's darker than the darkness of drawn shutters... You never tell me what day it is, or maybe I just keep forgetting, but it's still August, the dog days are coming to a close, I'm sensing something in the air of September, I don't know what, something of September, but I got there first, I screwed him over... You know what Tristano's seeing behind his eyelids? An August night from years ago, so many years ago, he's a boy sitting on his grandfather's knee, and they're out in the barnyard, and his grandfather knows so much about the sky and has promised to explain the sky to him that evening, his grandfather's a gruff man, he went all the way down to Sicily to shoot at the Bourbons and now he has a red shirt tucked away in a bureau smelling of camphor, everyone's very formal with him, except the boy, and his grandfather laughs with him a good deal, now he's taken hold of the boy's hand and is pointing it toward the starry sky, and he tells him to close one eye like he's aiming a musket, a bit more on high, he says, a bit more to sea – can you find it? – that's Orion, the north's behind us, what your nonno calls on high, understand, Ninototo? Behind Tristano's eyelids, the grandfather has an odd voice, he and the boy he's speaking to are one and the same person – so strange. But is it any stranger than the sky, with all those stars up there forever?... The things of this world are so old that by being old they're rejuvenated, as if they were tired of being old. We'll start in the west, his grandfather says – no – we'll start in the south, what your nonno calls to sea when he's talking to the cowherds. We'll start in the south because that's where you find Equuleus, the Little Horse, here, let me show you, follow my finger, at night I heard nonna sing you the lullaby of the dappled pony to make you fall asleep, I had a pony all dappled gray that counted clip-clops to the moon... there they are, those stars up there, they're called that for the story: the pony Mercury gave his friend as a gift, but the Greeks called him Hermes not Mercury, the Greeks discovered the stars first, because they came first, but the stars were there before anyone, now that direction, that's East, everything started there, in the East, everything comes from there, from that magnificent, ancient East where men understood things in the abstract, it's all been downhill from there, Ninototo, we haven't discovered a thing though we think we're so clever, but I'm getting off-track, let's get back to it, steady now, there, by the Little Horse, that's the Swan and that's the Swan's brightest star, Albireo, you can see what color it is through my telescope, it's orange, and nearby is Deneb, that's what the Arabs called it, which means tail... no, no – I'm wrong – Deneb's the brightest, it has a companion, a strange companion you can only see once every five years, a boy named Phaethon was transformed into that constellation, he was like Amilcare driving his ox cart, only Phaethon drove a sun cart, but he wasn't paying attention and he wound up in a ditch and the gods turned his cart into those stars you see. Now we'll shift some and you follow my finger, there's Capricorn, and Aquarius, they're faint stars, like graveyard candles, I can't see them, not without my telescope, but your eyes are good... how do I know these things by heart? Well, it's the same sky every summer, Ninototo, always the same sky, and I've studied it every summer of my life...

 

    These days everyone's so informal, you must have noticed, I find it brusque, overly familiar. I don't like it – it shows disrespect... I think when two people hold each other in high regard they should be more formal, it's more civilized, more respectful. And it creates the proper distance to make the other person understand that even if we know each other well, know each other intimately – our respective secrets – that we pretend we don't, that we don't know certain things, and we do this to make the other feel more comfortable, like when someone's confessed something important to you that he wouldn't tell anyone else and so you act a bit distracted, oh, not really, of course, you actually listened very carefully, but... well, it's like you already stopped thinking about it, you locked it away inside a secret compartment in your heart... Now that the time has come for us to say goodbye, now that it's time for me to take my leave, I want to be more formal with you. I'm sure you understand, it's not an insignificant detail… also because of what you'll write about me. Sound okay?


I think there's still a big fly in here, please, get it out, sir, I don't want that fly landing on my mouth after I've closed it. When you write this story, sir, when you turn it into a book, put your name on the cover, I don't want my own there, I don't want to be the one doing the telling, I want to be told… You wrote once that Tristano knew about fear, and I agreed. But real fear is something else again, that was a trifling kind of fear, a privileged, random fear, it could go badly, but it was also something you could get out from under… Real fear is when the hour's fixed and you know it's inevitable… that's a strange fear, unusual, something you experience once in a lifetime, never more, it's like vertigo, like throwing a window open onto nothing, and it's there that thought truly drowns, is obliterated. This, this is real fear… In a little while, when you no longer hear me breathing, throw the window wide, let in the light, the sounds of the living world. They belong to you, sir; silence belongs to me. And then leave right after, close the door and leave the corpse behind, it won't be me, I've already given Frau directions for disposing of it quickly… There's a religious love of death that's close to necrophilia, practically loving the corpse more than the living… A beautiful death… what nonsense, death's never beautiful, death is filthy – always, filthy – the denial of life… They say death's a mystery, but having existed at all is the greater mystery, this might seem banal, but it's really so mysterious… Take you and me, for instance, you know, finding ourselves here, in the same room, at this precise moment, it's very mysterious, or at least it's rather odd, wouldn't you say?… I thank you, sir… I'd like to give you another gift, you see that photograph on the dresser?, no, not the one on the other dresser, the dresser with the mirror, next to the glass bell, where the pendulum keeps moving the hands, because the hands keep going even after we stop, we may be the ones who invented clocks, but they obey a different master… I mean the one in the ebony frame, the one of the man from behind, walking down the shore… see those houses in the distance?… that's the town where my mother lived, my father's heading off to marry her, that's why he's dressed so elegantly though he's walking along the beach, after the ceremony he'll bring my mother here, to this house where I was born and that will soon be sold, after Frau dies… It's a beautiful photo, take it as a gift, use it in your book, it isn't Tristano, but it is a little, since it's his father… He has his back to us, as if he's saying goodbye, what I've been doing all these days with you, sir, and what I'm doing now for the last time… Check the clock, what time is it? That might sound foolish, but I want to know, it's the last thing I want to know… After all, like they say, tomorrow is another day.

This book has been with me a long while. Besides writing it at home, I composed it, in notebooks and in my thoughts, at the homes that dear friends put at my disposal. I thank these friends. It's superfluous to name them here: they know.

Thank you to Valentina Parlato who, with great precision and intelligence, typed out my handwritten notebooks and the parts I knew by memory that made up this book before it was a book.

A.T.

*Translator's note*

For the most part, English words that appear in italics were in English in the original novel.

There are a few poems that the narrator quotes which were translated into Italian; I have, at times, included others' English translations of these:

P. 29:  Heinrich Heine, "Die Lorelie," trans. A.S. Kline
P. 82:  C.P. Cavafy, "Long Ago," trans. Edmund Keeley and Philip Sherrard
P. 181: C.P. Cavafy, "Voices," trans. Edmund Keeley and Philip Sherrard

*Translator's Acknowledgments*

The translation of this novel was supported through residencies at the Banff International Centre for the Arts in Canada and the Casa delle traduzioni in Rome. Research for the translation was greatly aided through funding from the University of North Dakota and through a PEN/Heim Translation Fund Grant from the PEN America Center. I wish to thank Dr. Louise Rozier for her careful reading and insights about this novel and Dr. Charles Klopp for answering my many questions. I also wish to thank Jill Schoolman, publisher of Archipelago Books, for her devotion to Tabucchi, to literature in translation, and to translators. I dedicate this translation to the memory of my mother, Nancy Harris.

*archipelago books*

is a not-for-profit literary press devoted to
promoting cross-cultural exchange through innovative
classic and contemporary international literature
www.archipelagobooks.org